Death Wish of a Bad Girl

Amit Kumar Patra

It was 1990s, and India had overcome a monotonous economy and pushed its availability to welcome entities which held a great desire to make trade with us for mutual benefits. Growth always has a bitter path to follow and consequences are collateral damage and history remains an innocent victim of it. In the power corridor, many charlatan governments took the oath to make India proud but their words are clever attempts to establish their government. That resulted in the death of a visionary leader Mr. Rajiv Gandhi in the year of 1991. The game of bloodbath didn't stop there. The footstep of the blood-smeared history walked to the day of 12th March 1993. By that time the turmoil between Mandeer, Mandal, and Market gives an advantage to the Mumbai underworld to establish their secularism through mass murder. India never forgot the day of sequence Mumbai blast. That day another unusual thing happens at Leelavati hospital, Mumbai. The time was exactly midnight; wall clock in the corridor rang. With it, a little nap Raghab was headed broke. He looked around hesitated. The door of room number 305 opened and a doctor comes in hurry. Raghab looked up at him. The doctor still stood there and looked him for confirmation. He waved his head slightly and approved. The doctor gasped and walked into that room again.Raghab suddenly stood from his place and walk straight and rapidly to the lavatory. Splashes of water hit his face and yet he continuously hit a few more drops of cold water onto his face. Finally, he stopped. He can see the disappointment on his face, looking at his expression in the mirror gasped and finally closing his eyes not wanting to see his face again. It reminds him of a few days ago when he brought his wife with critical labour pain and the doctor gave him the option to save only one life. Both expressions of fear and confusion reflected from the wrinkles that appeared on his forehead. He thought all day and night his heart conjured in fear of losing both. The day of 12th March 1993 Raghab have to take his final decision about who he wanted to save. He tucks a leave from the office and spends all day at the hospital. By 3:00 pm, something happened at outdoor, quarrels, screaming, and pathetic noise of people coming from outside. He was curious and went to the window to find the reason. The whole hospital was smeared in blood, and people shouted in melancholy. Countless dead bodies are at the hospital gallery. He went downstairs, for giving a helping hand to the medical staff. Tuck a side of the stretcher and tried to move it out from the ambulance. Suddenly he stood still, his eyes broad in fear. That was the dead body of his dear friend Raman. They work together as a lawyer for the House of royal judicial farm. He was seated on a bench near room number 305. His mind was jammed. The corridor was full of rush. Escalation of dead bodies and injured people are continuously come and goes through the way all day. On the one side, he can't forget the blood-smeared dead body of his friend, and another hand he has to take a decision about whom he wants alive, his wife or the child. The time was making his situation worst. A dizziness appeared before his eyes and closed slowly and slowly. Something like darkness all around. A sudden tension in his breath and he came back to the conscious world. Raghab was still standing near the sink and the lavatory door was opened. Something rushes through his body and he ran with that speed. The doctor was standing out of room 305 and saw Raghab hurrying toward him. He looked cold expression of the doctor's for a moment and went into the room. At one side upon the bed, his wife Smita was unconsciously sleeping, and behind in a cradle dead body of a small baby was waiting for his father's last acquaintance. Raghab tuck his slow and resisting steps toward the cradle. Moved slowly with a blow of wind. He bends his knees down. The face was exactly as he imagined. Round, pointed nose, and bright skin. His hands are trembling while touching the soft skin of the baby. His small hands and tiny fingers were very adorable. Raghab kissed the fleshy cheek and looked conform to the face. Tears came out of his eyes and started sobbing. A few drops of tears rolled down and fall upon the forehead of the baby. Something happened magically. A slight movement in the body. Raghab felt it and looked thorough. Another drop of tear dropped on forehead of the baby. Suddenly a cry hollered and a tiny tongue come out from the mouth and the mouth was opened wide. Plenty of air breathed in. Stopped for a moment and again started crying flapping tiny legs and hands. Raghad can't believe his eyes. Put the baby carefully in the cradle, ran out of the room towards the doctor's office.

***

Hi I'm Raman, a child resurrected from his father's melancholy tears. My father Mr. Raghab singh Ray and my mother Mrs. Smita Ray had a conception that their dear friend Raman Jain sole was in my body so they name me after him. The day I was born very unusual but concepts and consequences are a part of life. As to follow that we moved to Odisha, native and dearer to my parents. My mom and dad were from Bhubaneswar. By that time Odisha was not developed as compared to other states so fall in love at a young age was a committable offense according to the conservative elders' thought, my parents not only loved, they did marry which make them a felony for their natives. After my birth, everything was solved. We not only came back, but my father joined Ray's judicial farm. A respective and only legal advising company established by my grandfather Mr. Surjit Singh Ray. My grandfather and his company had a great influence on the judicial business of Odisha but he didn't use it full-fledged. Upper hand my father travelled and worked in many reputed and influenced law farms around India and got great exposure working with magnificent mentors. He knew sooner or after Odisha will go through the marketing competition and great churning are going to happen and the evolution of the market and the societal concept was inevitable. Slow and steady my father took the lifeline of Ray Judicial firm. My grandfather never used the influences and the connections he achieved through his services but my father does. When he was a young lawyer in Mumbai he learned many tricks from his superiors now time for utilization. He wanted to make his business an invincible organization so that in the future the firm can resist the changes. From the beginning of their relationship, my mother was fond of his visionary thought process. She tucks all responsibility for the house and me. I was a shy, introvert, and silent kid who never leaves the site of his mother. My body was looking like made of straw and illness was a nightmare that never leaves me. Rarely do I go out of my house and the window seat of my room was the only connection between me to the real world. Days are passed by and under the guidance of my mother education began at home. Sooner I got my place of amusement, the library. My grandfather was a book lover and his library decorum spokes fluently his sickness for the books. That genetic approach was transferred in me as well. I was four years old, and my grandfather brought me Gitanjali. One of the finest crafts done by the greatest of all time writer Mr. Rabindranath Tagore. Days are passing on and my friendship with the library was more incredible. The books gave me proper visions of the outer world, like time travel sometime books take me to Paris, and another time I was travelling with Aladdin and his adventurous consequences. Finally, my mother was happy for me but that didn't go well with my father. He was a practical approaching man and according to him; Raghab: "Reading and acquiring knowledge from books gives a brief idea, it is the practical experiences which give us the clarity, built us a decision maker."

Those words are too heavy for me to understand but one thing I understood my days of paradise are over. 'When one gate closed another gate of opportunity opened'. According to my grandfather's opinion. The gates of Sand Joseph school were sure opened. It was my ancestral school. My grandfather and father graduated and built their milestone. The worst part was the school authority settled high hopes for me accordingly. I remembered the preamble. Standing in front of the rust old-looking gate and the janitor Ram bhai. He was a black fat man having a great ideological moustache. He opened the gates with a unique smile and my journey with the school was begun. The days went well at the beginning. Preparing school bags, shining shoes, mentioning hygiene and the best part was waiting for the bus. Someone says happiness is a freckle friend so it was to me. I was good in scores and that was the reason I was a highlighted student in school. Teachers always praised me for my good handwriting and obedience was the factor they were amazed at. Unknowingly I ruined the ambition of a few fellow mates. Ronith Dash was one of them. He was a fat and mischievous student in our class. He pursues only one goal to be famous in school. Snatching others' lunch boxes, beating fellow mates for amusement, and misbehaving with the girls are his daily routine work. The trouble was I got his attention. I was in fifth standard at that time and for the first time I talked to him in school bus.

Ronith: "Hey Raman come here I saved a seat for you."

Raman: "Thanks, Ronith I'm fine on my own."

Ronith: "Are you?"

He spoke threateningly and caught my arms tight and pulls near his seat. He gave a cunt smile looking at my face. Swallowed a bit in fear and the juggling sound of my throat were audible to him. He looked me like enjoyed the fear on my face.

Ronith: "Don't be afraid Raman, I'm always on your side, can't you see!"

He offered me a toffee with a clever smile.

Raman: "Yes of course."

That fear getting more impulse on me.

Ronith: "Look brother you help me... I help you, you go trespassing me, and it will be a problem. The order should be mentioned. Yes, brother!"

Raman: "Yes understood."

The school bus arrived at the gate and with a static flow stopped. I felt relieved and stood from my seat. A thick hand was on my shoulder. I looked back, that was Ronith again. Looking at me with assurance. All classmates entered the classroom and were seated according to the designated places. The exam began after five minutes, classroom was silent.

Ronith: "Hsss... Hssss..... hey!!! Hey!!! Raman?"

I was involved with the answer sheet and that voice continuously disturbed me. Finally looked back. Ronit was there and continuously pampering me for help. I leaned aside and he started following my answer sheet. Someone was marking from a distance.

Paridhee Ma'am: "Ronith.....!"

Ronith: "Yes, Paridhee Ma'am."

She walked faster and snatched his answer paper and gave me a dared look. I looked at her like guilty and back to writing my things. The invigilator walked away from the place and back of her Ronith. Requesting as well as accusing her of ruing his exam. The exam hall was all in silence, everyone involved in their writing, Teachers are walking around looking cautious and with it my pen stopped scratching the paper. Looked up at the wall clock. There were still ten minutes left. A smile on my face and my eyes are busy reviewing the answer sheets. The exam went well but the exam with my life was just begun. It was very calm and satisfying Ronith was not near me. I collected the school bag and went to the bus, settled on my seat. It was a while since I was looking out the window. Something happened in slow motion, before I could address, Ronith approached and started beating me. When I come to a position to know him and his fellow gang flew from the place. Bruises are in my elbow, forehead and lips fragile. It was just beginning he tucked many attempts to take me down. I feared to go school and even feared talking about it with my parents. For Ronith I was a toy for amusement and tuck every chance to conjure the class by setting me an example. I started spending my time more lonely. The fear was so far in me I wasn't even able to share my feelings with my family. The only thing that supported me in all these years was literature. It was in defined routine reading fiction stories every day in library. My life was running up and downs then she came! After summer vacation first day of my seventh standard. The bus was fully crowded. All my fellow mates are happy and busy exchanging their experiences. Just with an unaware expression I was seating at a corner, looking down to the street like everything was new to me. The bus was stopped at a station and a few students are jumped into. Nothing bothers me. I was reminded the day before summer vacation. Our school librarian;

Gupta Sir: "Raman you are making it harsh. Look at the children at your age; they have plans to explore the vacation in their own way. What are you going to do?"

I have a glancing smile to answer him. He looked at me worried and busies himself assigning the books I was urged. The bus was stopped and I understood I have reached the gate of the school. Many of my friends have ugly faces. I felt disagreed; school was like a second home to me. Someone pushed me from the stairs of the bus and I landed on the ground badly.

Ronith: "How are you, buddy? You don't know I missed you a lot. After all, my hands need to work on something."

Speaking of it Ronith walked near and gave a demonic famish look and his cunt smile was enough to conjure me. My head was down like a slave and my hands are shaking.

Raman: "Not now.... not now. You can manage Raman, you can do it."

I was speaking it to myself continuously and collecting the books from the floor into my bag. A helping hand forwarded. I looked up, what a gorgeous beauty. Her eyes are so clean and confident. My heart was pounding, breathing goes disturbed as my mind. Something shaking freaking me out. Her expressions are much focused like everything went slow around me. In the middle of it, a thick hand was moving into action. But sad she not only intercepted it but jolted a slap to him. Suddenly a fearful silence spread around like all activities are stopped. Ronith was silent for a moment; his hand was on his red thick cheek. A moment later few drops of tears run down and he cried funnily. Suddenly the situation became funny and motivates us to laugh. I settled my school bag and stood, but before I could thank her she left. The news spread like fire. All school suddenly wants to know about her including me. It was 11:00 'O'clock and I was at the library waiting in the row submitting the books.

Librarian: "Hmmm.... you look blushing boy."

Raman: "And why is that for Gupta sir."

Suddenly my face got jittery, my eyes are nervous and my cheeks got red with a shy smile. Gupta sir was giving a conform look on me.

Librarian: "Finally......something is going to happen good with you my boy."

Raman: "What does that mean sir?"

Librarian: "Nothing dear... Just never let your feelings die who knows she may be a life-changing moment for you."

I was shocked and looked that way. Gupta sir was very normal and looked directly into my eyes like an experienced man. A sweet pain was suffering my heart, which I don't want to show anyone. He found it. Saving my eyes from him I moved quickly from the library. Walked slowly and stubbornly towards class. Before entering into it; Class teacher: "Raman where have you been, come in it's already late dear."

Raman: "Sorry ma'am I was at the library submitting books."

Class teacher: "Okay don't waste any more time and go find your seat."

Raman: "Yes.... ma'am."

I entered the classroom and while going to my seat looked at Ronith, he was glaring at me like hungry wolf. I swallowed a bit in fear and settled in my seat. After a terrific morning finally had a positive feeling skimming inside the classroom. Principal ma'am entered!

Principal ma'am: "Students please sit down, we are here for an announcement that soon our new library is going to install and for that few social events are going to hold on. Please confirm your participation."

She was about to go but stopped near the entrance gate. Returned to the classroom.

Principal ma'am: "Students there is another announcement remaining. Please welcome, Miss. Akriti panda. Miss. Akriti, please stand up at your place."

From the middle row, a girl stood and walk slowly to the front. She was looking directly to my eyes. Her eyes are so clear and beautiful. Suddenly I felt uncomfortable. My face was all sweaty and redness appeared on my cheeks, heart was pounding like a steam engine. Before I lost control eyes are closed. It was a very different feeling never happened before. She went to the front and stood among the teachers. The class was whispering about the morning incident. One thing satisfies me. I'm not the only one who hiding faces. Ronith had suffered the way I was but he was terrified of her. I looked up. Her little bold eyes are looking at everyone and at the end; her eyes are set on me. I behaved cowardly. That was so uneasy experience.

***

I stopped reading and released a long breath. When looked beyond, plenty of people are looking at me with respective expressions. A smile appeared on my lips.

Raman: "Thanks for your humble attention. My part of the play is over for now."

Carrying a humble expression I walked down from the stage. A smile of gratitude was on my face. Following the moment a lady walked to the stage with her support stick. Her skin looked white, and hands are shaking, walking like she was an old lady. Head was bald and a graceful smile on her face. She settled at the place very carefully. A man from backstage helped her.

Akriti: "Hi, I'm Akriti, sorry I'm not in an appropriate state to speak so please cooperate with my situation and listen to me."

There was a slow sound of whispering surrounding, many questions on the faces of audience. Ignoring them she harrumphed like preparing for reading. I saw her bold eyes are ready to dive into the deep ocean of words. She opened the book and narrow down her eyes to the pages.

That was my first day at school. After summer vacation my mom shifted to Bhubaneswar. The school bus was plenty full of gossip and transactions of vacation experiences. I was silently looking at all of them and listening to them. My eyes stopped on one particular boy who was looking outside the window and a satisfied silence on his face. Later on, I found him in class. I can't stop staring at him. Finally, he looked at me. Something was different in that eyes, something common but not so common. I thought we will be friends. A few days went in school I made new friends. Collected information about that boy. He was Raman, one of the richest kids. I got more fascinated and dig deep. He was an introvert and shy person. Very shy but brilliant. He was among the top four in class. All over he was a package of appreciation and the total opposite of me. I need more to learn about him and then it happens! Miracles existed only in wonderland but guess what? I'm the new neighbour of that brilliant lad. I was alighted from the taxi and looked around the new abate; suddenly my eyes went to a window of neighbour house where a boy was sitting silently and looked straight at me. A cunt smile appeared on my lips. All day my mom was busy shifting the luggage and after assisting her I played my game.

We went to his house. A beautiful garden at the beginning and a huge door after that. We hit the bell. A pretty lady opened the door. I guess she was his mother and behind her was him. Stood silently and looked at me like some imposter I was.

Anita: "Hello I'm Anita and she is my daughter Akriti. We just moved here today. I hope we didn't disturb you, ma'am!"

Smita: "Hello, I'm Smita Ray, good to see you both. Please come in. I'm looking forward to giving a visit to your house. It's a long time since the last owner left."

In the middle of that, I walked slowly and touched her feet, and said "namaste". She put both of her hands on my shoulder and looked affectionate.

Smita: "Your daughter is so pretty Mrs. Anita."

Anita: "So pleasant of you Mrs. Smita. And he must be your son. Hi dear, what is your name?"

I walked a few steep back and hide behind mom.

Smita: "Never mind Mrs. Anita, he is not friendly. It will take time for him to be an acquaintance."

My eyes are exactly on him. He looked nervous. It was so funny. I walked forward to begin the conversation. He looked furious and redness was on his face. It was good enough for laugh out loud.

Anita: "I'm sorry Mrs. Smita she is the opposite of your son. Talkative and acquainting new people is her specialty."

Both of the ladies laughed badly. I looked them but didn't understand the reason. Leaving us out there they went into the drawing room. He still looked at me differently and a miracle happened.

Raman: "Hi... I... like to thank you the other day you saved me from Ronith."

Appreciation was ecstatic. Boy got the manners, impressive.

Grandpa: "Finally you found a friend Golu. It's wonderful. Don't you like to introduce your friend to me?"

That was a thick and heavy voice. We turned to the place. An old man was walking to us and a beautiful cane in his hand proves his superiority. I realized he must be Raman's grandfather.

Grandpa: "May I know your name dear?"

Akriti: "Akriti,"

I said and did Namaste. His face was glowing with happiness.

Grandpa: "So Akriti please tell me dear what you think about stories?"

Akriti: "They are wonderful."

Grandpa: "So are you interested joining us in our small cult?"

Akriti: "Cult?"

Grandpa smiled meticulously and hints me to follow him. I was curious and looked at Raman. He still stood hesitant at a distance. I think he might be not a ready-forward person. But I can't refuse grandpa so then I walked steadily following him. After walking a few steep ahead he stopped near a door. He opened it and walked in. I was following him. I looked wider around. It was a huge library. The walls are surrounded by racks full of books and the place was preserved very pretty and looked classic.

Akriti: "So this is the reason behind the extraordinary boy."

I was thinking.

Grandpa: "So are you ready for story time Akriti."

Akriti: " I'm not a good storyteller grandpa."

Grandpa: "Aoo... this boy, he always had qualities."

I looked amazed at Raman. His eyes went down and a shy smile was on his lips. We were both seated at the audience site and he stood in front of us and a book was in his hand. I never imagined behind the shy personality Raman was extremely talented and the way he did elaborate the story I enjoyed a lot. It felt so real and addicted to it.

✳✳✳

At present, Akriti stopped reading and looking at the audience, her breathing gone heavy and a spot boy walk immediately to her with a bottle of water. The audience was curious and feared too. Raman walked to the stage and grab her in his arms carefully. She looked at him and smiled. She saw a reflection of his childhood face.

Raman: "Are you fine dear?"

Akriti: "Yes, Golu I'm totally fine. Just my tongue got dry."

He tucks the book from her hands and seated next behind. They looked at each other and smiled like a time travel is to begin. With them, the audience buckled up to dive into the ocean of stories.

When Grandpa approached the library I felt hesitant because he was the only person in my life who always praised my creativity. I don't know what his intention was but Akriti showed her interest in it so I can't resist. Trust me I was nervous when I saw her beautiful eyes looking at me like waiting for magic to happen. I closed my eyes and took a deep breath. Pretend as if she was not there in the library and started reading. After the end of my story session, I closed the book and the first face I looked was her. There was an intense expression in her eyes. That gave me more nervousness. Overall my first impression on her went well. That night after dinner I went to bed soon. The last thing I remember was her face. It was midnight and I was in deep sleep, slow but a continuous sound of opening and closing of the window set me awake. A shadow immediately entered into the room. The way it come to me was very conjuring.

Raman: "Akriti you....!"

She was smiling looking at my furious cry-baby face. I was so confused seeing her trespassing in my bed room at an indefinite time of the midnight.

Raman: "What are you doing here in the middle of the night?"

She smiled again and handed me 'The Post Office'. I saw the novel and looked at her face with a questionable expression.

Akriti: "I was trying to sleep but there are a lot of mosquitoes in my new home. So if you read a few lines for me I will go and sleep."

She explained her stupidity crisp and clear. I looked out to the window and to the pipeline which was connected to my window, gasped and looked at her. That puppy face expression on her was still fresh. The demand can't be avoided. I tuck the book from her hand and like a good girl she jumps on the bed and looked eagerly at my face. I grabbed the chair next to me and started reading. I never knew she was just not impressed got obsessed with my talent for reading stories. Morning walked into my room, the cold light of son was making the nature glow and the sweet voice of little birds bring me back from my dreams. Suddenly I got alert and looked around. There was no one in the room. I was sleeping on a chair and a blanket was surrounding me. My eyes went to the bed. There was a book and the pages are flapping continuously in the direction of the window. I looked there, the window was open and the sound of cold winter air was very soothing, struggled a bit but got out of the blanket, went to the window. The doors are making noise as last night. I smiled funny.

Smita: "Golu go get ready, aren't you going to school today? I want you ready in ten minutes."

Raman: "Yes...yes mom I will be there. Don't worry I won't be late."

Within an hour, I was at the doorstep of my house. A different energy was in my eyes. For the first time, felt different. A spark of some intention that was only dedicated to her. The school bus arrived and I get on it. For a moment confused. She was not in there, I thought.

Akriti: "Golu.... come I saved a seat for you."

I followed the voice and saw she was in the middle row waiting for me. My face was blushing. It was a VIP feeling for me. She tucks her bag out from behind and pulled my hand to sit next to her. I felt flattered but not for long. Other boys were looking at me in anger and jealousy was on their faces. That was just the beginning. With day's most of the time spent with her. She was beautiful and daring and possesses every approach which helped her to become a popular girl in school.

Someone got hurt by her popularity but he can't help it. Ronith himself fall in one-sided love trap with her. I was the true victim of his imbecilic attempts. Not only he, many boys wanted to be with her and I was their hope and messenger. With time our friendship grows younger and deeper. I had tried to express my feelings for her but Akriti always tuck me as a friend. Hope someday..... Someday she may understand my feelings. Until that day I will be her best buddy. That was usual like all days I was at lawn and enjoying reading the book. Like me my classmates were playing and enjoying their time as appropriate they wanted. A shadow appeared before the book and I looked up.

Rashi: "I thought you are in some other world. Thanks, you are not lost."

In return, I just smiled at her. Rashi Mathur was her name and she was one of the famous girls in our school. She tucks the next place behind me. I felt fishy and looked at her like for the first time I saw her. She was constantly looking at my face, something she was impressed about me!

Rashi: "You never told me that you are a skilled storyteller."

Raman: "What?"

Looked her awkward. It was shocking no one ever knows about my affection for literature. I saw around, boys and girls are looking at me in different ways. I was about to go but...

Class teacher: "Raman come principal ma'am wants to meet you?"

Principal ma'am: "I never knew that we have a talented boy like you, Raman. Akriti did share the audio recordings of your story sessions. In-person, I like to say they are wonderful. I enjoyed each personally. It was like you are a character in the story and....."

She suddenly stopped in the middle of the conversation and searched among the documents. A smile above her lips and in that delight, she gave an envelope. I looked at it for a while and then tuck it. There was a detailed brief about the event; it was an inauguration of the library which was newly constructed. As a guest of honour district IAS officer and deputy chief minister was going to attend. On behalf of the occasion a reading session to be held and I'm to leading the session. The situation was both mixture of happiness and fear for me. Akriti did understand my imbecilic expression and walked with me out of the principal's office. The envelope was in my hand and my head was down and I walked until reached the backyard of the school. There was an old Banyan tree in the middle of the garden and my regular place. I went to my appropriate place and seated. There was a soothing silence. Still looking at the envelope. Within a few time, Akriti walked towards me. I saw her; she gave me a numb smile.

Raman: "Are you creasy Akriti?"

Akriti: "No!"

Raman: "Then why you do this to me?"

Akriti: "What I did?"

Raman: "You know......"

Tears are rolling out from my eyes and my shoulders are down. I was hopeless and looking her to solve the issue she has began.

Akriti: "You know Golu why I always admire you?"

Raman: "Because we are good friends and we share our secrets"

Akriti: "No."

Akriti: "You have a very kind heart and want to see everyone happy."

Raman: "What is the point of saying Akriti?"

Akriti: "To see everyone happy you disgrace the talent within you."

Akriti: "You are very lucky because you are a creative person and among few who can able to do which no one can do."

Just looking at her mesmerized. The Akriti I knew was a spoiled girl. This one was something.... something unexplainable. Every word from her mouth was inspiring and gave a boon to my inner strength. A feeling of cosmic strength which never felt before. For the first time, I felt that in keeping people happy I forgot myself and she is the girl who was aware from the beginning.

Raman: "This is the moment Raman say it.... don't think just speak your feeling. She is the one..... She is the only love of your life."

My inner voice was hammering my heart and a sweet aching was thrilled all over my body. I was in the edge to speak those magical words.

Raman: "Akriti I want to say something?"

Akriti: "Yes!!!"

She was looking at me pointing her honking eyes like trying to read my mind. I swallowed in fear and looked at her face for a moment and tuck a deep breath.

Raman: "I'm ready for the story session."

Akriti: "Yes....yes that's my boy my Golumolu, I knew it."

Suddenly she got ecstatic and kissed both of my cheeks and ran. I was standing still 'What just happened she kissed my cheeks.'

✳✳✳

We back to the present time. People are anxiously looking to the stage. Spotlight was dimmed and gradually the brightness of the gallery was improved. The audience row seems to be disappointed.

Raman: "Sorry to keep you all waiting for the next day. We will right back at this exact time and will know did Raman propose Akriti. If did then what next?"

After the announcement slowly people moved towards the exit door and their delightful face was very satisfying to see. Akriti was looking at my face and put her hand slowly on mine. I looked at her and grinned. She smiled ailing. I gasped and tuck her hands carefully. Two spot boys came down to help her. Thanks to her support stick we made through the exit door. The outdoors was so cloudy and thunder was cracking. Two drops of water fell on my cheeks. Looking at my face she smiled. That day in school rain welcome me like want to share my happiness. My classmates are eager to go on the bus but I was walking slowly like enjoying the rainy moment. Akriti. As always she saved a seat for me. Throughout the journey, I saw her. She was so normal and calm like nothing happened. Finally, I conclude that the incident was just an ecstatic friendly moment. That night I can't sleep. Seating at the study table doing something. A sound from the side of the window. I was not amazed it was her. Without showing any attention I keep busy doing my work.

Akriti: "Hmmm..... Poem...... good.... good. Save it for Tuesday. You can use this in your story session and trust me the audience will be surprised when they know you are multi-talented."

Akriti: "There may be a chance that some news channel may broadcast you. Glory and fame will be at your door step. Hey..... Raman, you may find a beautiful girlfriend, and all of your classmates envy you."

Eyes got moist in tears and pen was stopped writing. Few drops were fall on the diary and bruised the letters.

Finally anger consumes over mind and next instant the diary was in the dust-bin.

Akriti: "Are you mad Golu? It's a master craft.... if you want to disgrace your talent then stop praising it."

She was really mad at me.

Raman: "After school, I was so happy. I got my first opportunity to represent my talent. Before I could understand Mom arrived and slapped me."

Akriti: "Aunty!!!!!..... Why?"

Raman: "Mom did a pact with me that she will support my creativity only if I keep it within me."

Akriti: "That's insane."

Raman: "I know Akriti that's insane."

Akriti: "Why she is behaving that outrage?"

Finally she got the diary out of dustbin and seating next to me focused on problem.

Raman: "My mom..... She was a brilliant mathematician in her college and the topper one. She has an ambition to pursue her carrier in math but eventually, destiny demands differently. When she had me her first intention was to see me as a mathematician."

Akriti: "So!"

Raman: "Remain you can judge by yourself, Akriti."

She gasped.

Akriti: "So.... what next?"

I gave a meticulous smile to her question. She gave me a confused look as trying to read my expressions.

***

Within a moment I woke up and found the car arrived at the apartment and looked behind. Akriti was still sleeping. Her bald head and wrinkled ailing face felt me unhappy, but what to do no one can deny God's judgment.

Akriti: "Don't look me in that way. I don't like that expression on your face Golu."

Akriti: "I'm not going to die that easy."

I laughed at her statement and we both alighted from the car. Drizzling rain and the slow cold air changed the climate. Akriti was severing in cold. I brought her carefully to the house.

Akriti: "Dear, I'm dying. It is time now you should look for a better one. Someone who can.....!!!!"

Frowned in the middle of the conversation.

Raman: "Stop there Akriti we had discussed it already."

Akriti: "You are a 27-year-old eligible man and now a celebrity author. Do you like to spend remain of your life alone?"

Spoke gibberish.

Raman: "I will never be alone. I have you, Akriti."

Akriti: "For how long? You need to accept the truth Golu."

Both of our eyes blurred in tears and we hugged. At some point within our hearts, we already accepted the fait. The weather outside gone worst at night. We thought tomorrow's session may be postponed but morning welcomed us with a smiley sunshine. When we arrived at the gallery our eyes were mesmerized. The gallery was houseful and the audience was anxiously waiting for us. We both smiled looking at each other. I did realize a boon of motivation possessed her body and she was moving her cane faster to ride onto the stage. After we settled she tucks the book and turned to the next page.

I don't know why he gave that clever look but one thing that I confirmed about Raman was the tears in his eyes were for me. Finally, the day of the event arrived. The school library was houseful. Teachers, parents, and chief guests looking towards the closed red screen. I was backstage with Raman. For the first time in my life, I was so nervous but he seems usual.

Akriti: "Golu, are you nervous?"

Raman: "Yes!"

Akriti: "I'm just asking?"

Raman: "I know Akriti. Your worries are for my parents. They are an audience and I need to be cautious."

Akriti: "Yes!!!"

Raman: "Trust me everything going to be fine."

In return, I waved my head and looked at him ahead towards the stage. It was the creepiest day for me. My heart was pounding with every step he embarks towards stage.

Raman: "Hello I'm Raman and I am the person who is your entertainment guru for today."

A smiley expression appeared from the audience.

Raman: "Let me tell you I'm here appointed to tell you a story which can entertain you but eventually I learned that is not sufficient. There are a lot of grown people unaware of the power of words and literature. For them, Literature is just subject schools and colleges are wasting their time. For me, Literature nurtures my emotion and gives me the advantage to think like an empathetic."

The audience was listening to his words very carefully. I was among them just behind his mother and looking at her expressions. At that moment someone put his hand on my shoulder. I looked to my next behind. Grandpa grinned at me and gave me thumbs up. In return, I smiled. Smita Aunty was looking at everything. She so frowned. Sudden courageous claps among the audience gave the distraction and I escaped. The storytelling event went well and beyond expectations. As I said many reporters clicked his photos and many audiences liked his storytelling talents. Within an instant, he became the hero of the school. Teachers are proud to put his name on their lips. I was happy for Grandpa. He always wanted him to be known for the skills he possessed. Eventually, everything went well except our friendship. There are a lot of social attentions and attempts are working together. We are in the middle of the ninth standard. Our social priorities are changed according to our family prospects. Raman was busy preparing for abroad. His parents wanted his further education in America. Smita Aunty set her high hopes to build him a greatest of all time mathematicians and Raghab uncle wanted him a businessman, a bright future for the Rye law firm. But what he wants to become no one bothered to ask. By that time Grandpa was started ailing and looking to his health condition he tucks a permanent retirement from the business. Now he stays all day at home, and every day at 06:00 pm Raman to entertain him reading novels. I can say the most difficult time for Smita aunty. The time was changing for me too. After the death of my father, my mother was alone for a long time and she accepted the destiny decided by God. Those days it was very difficult for a single working mother to take care of a growing girl but together we became best friends. We have a ritual, every night before sleep mom gave me a head massage, comb my hairs and I share my whole day story and one name was common with in 'Golu'. My universe was always around him and his are always with me. Unknowingly we are two bodies and one sole and mom understood that for sure, which I didn't understand was mom needs a soul mate who can kill her loneliness too. Like the other days that were usual, sky was clear and birds were had back to their nest like me going back to home, unusual mom never left the main door opened. Bad thoughts hitting my mind and slowly I put the school bag at the main door and walked carefully to the hall. Few moaning sounds from the bedroom. Mom was enjoying sex with a man on bed. Both were involved in each other's like wanted to be together forever. It can't be tolerated for me, only option was disruption so I did. I walked to the main door and hit the bell continuously.

Anita: "Are you out of your mind Akriti, stop pushing that bell."

She was angry and looked in chaos.

Akriti: "Yes mom I'm out of my mind."

I said that rebelliously and pushed the door wide opened. That man was standing behind it.

Kartic: "Hell Akriti I'm Kartic."

Saying that he gave a chocolate. By that time mom looked very anxious, I don't want to ruin her happiness. She looked fulfilled after a long time.

Akriti: "Thanks."

Slow and steady my life started narrating a picture of adulthood and problems are also like that. We entered to the tenth standard and with it, the rate race began. Most of my classmates had plans for their future. Raman, well he was the busiest adult in our class. That was not his fault. He belongs to a very reputed family which a kid like me can only imagine and I think these rich kids always have the legacy issue. Smita Aunty restricted him to meet and spending time with me. According to her, I was the reason to spoil his mind and corrupt his thought process using the word passion. These days Raman was look more like machine enchanted man than a heart-full passionate glowing one. His grandfather was the only reason we are still in touch. My life was not so far easy as it once. It was recently discovered mom was pregnant, guess who was the father 'Kartic uncle'. In a few months they both going to be married and we are all together happy family again. That was what my mom expected. It was a Saturday evening and I was too tired and like a lame walked to the school bus. My mind was bewildered. A lot of thoughts were running in and out.

Raman: "Hey Akriti stop.... sss..... stop."

I stand still looking at him until he comes near.

Raman: "Let's go to the principal and...."

Akriti: "But why Golu?"

Raman: "I saw Arun sir in the classroom with you. The way he behaved is not appropriate. We should complain it to the principal ma'am."

Akriti: "And then what is going to happen? Do you ever try to understand what is going around me.... ever Golu?"

I was angry and depressed of loneliness I can't control my tears and hiding my face ran into the bus. Raman was standing still looking at me running away. He was worried but I don't want to be a burden on him. The night I can't sleep. The incident with Arun sir still hunting my thoughts. Suddenly I heard a sound on the closed window, I was threatened by fear. Tuck a stick and then opened the letch carefully.

The outside was dark and Raman was standing in front of me with a flashlight in his hand. He looked terrific.

Akriti: "Have you gone mad Golu? What are you doing in the middle of the night?"

He laughed looking at my imbecilic face.

Raman: "Look who is saying..... don't you remember you are the one who always trace pass my bedroom."

Akriti: "Those are childish days, now we are adults."

She said it awkward.

Raman: "What is the story of Arun sir?"

The smile from my face vanished. He was still looking directly into my eyes.

Akriti: "Why are you still out there?"

Raman: "Ooo..... now you see. I thought you're never going to ask."

The night was so young and the moon was looking at both of us through the window. For a moment our eyes are mate. There was a deep intention in it like wanting to say something.

Anita: "Akriti why didn't you sleep yet?"

Mom suddenly entered the room. She was horrified finding Raman out there.

Anita: "Raman, what are you doing here at this late hour?"

We both are not prepared for this situation.

Akriti: "Mom... He is here for his math notes. Golu told me earlier this morning but I forgot."

Raman: "Yes Aunty..... Math notes. I need it urgently that's why I'm here."

Anita: "No... Problem Golu. You are welcome anytime."

Raman: "Yes, Aunty."

Mom was about to walk out of the room.

Raman: "Aunty I'm here to discuss something with her."

Mom turned to us and looked at Raman suspicious.

Raman: "Aunty what I want to tell you is a little awful thing. I did saw something today at school."

Her expression got worst. I think she started to read his expressions. I wanted to stop Raman but it was too late now.

Raman: "You know Arun sir!"

Anita: "Yes, Golu he is your sports teacher."

Raman: "Yes.... aunty."

Raman: "Today after class as usual I was in the library reading something. There was a window near me and occasionally my eyes went by and saw Akriti was busy reading something alone. I smiled and again busy with my books. Five minutes after I looked again, Arun air standing near her desk."

Akriti: "Stop Golu not a single word."

I said it irresistibly.

Akriti: "Few days before Arun sir caught me red-handed in the backyard of the school smoking cigarette with my friends. I thought he might tuck me to the principal but he didn't. From that day he started flirting with me."

I started crying like there was a pain deep down in me. Raman and Mom both came and hold my hands to tell me that I was not alone.

Akriti: "I never knew he will go that far. This evening there was a vacant class. I was the only one there, writing my assignment and then he came."

Mom was looking at me and her melancholy eyes can't hold tears.

Akriti: "In the beginning, he was talking with me friendly so do I but after a few moments he put his hands on my shoulder like enjoying the touch and leaned a little front, he was smelling my hair.... after that as Golu saw he was moving his hands on my back and front. I felt uneasy and pushed him out of my site and ran away."

Golu was happy of my gutsy and fair approach and mom stood in my favour. I learned that I'm not alone after a long time.

∗∗∗

Peon: "I'm sorry ma'am for the interruption but it's urgent. Akriti and Raman both of you come to the principal cabin."

We both looked at each questionably and a fear was induced in our intention. Following the man entered to the principal office. Kartic uncle and a policeman were seated out there. A moment after that Arun sir entered the office, the environment got tensed. Principal Ma'am gave him an awful look. He understood the situation and after finding the policeman he got panicked.

Arun Sir: "Ma'am this girl is no good for our school. She is influencing her classmate's bad things, smoking cigarettes. I caught her a few days ago at the backyard of our school."

Principal Ma'am was listening to his arguments till the end.

Principal ma'am: "Then why don't you report to me Arun sir."

Arun sir: "Ma'am……. I thought that I can handle the situation by myself."

Policeman: "Can you elaborate us how you did tuck the situation under control, Mr. Arun?"

He was silent. The policeman stood from his place and walked near him. Silence for a moment and after that he jolted a slap. The situation was unavoidable. He understood now he had no chance to defend himself and sit silently like that on the floor. He was angry and wanted revenge desperately. The case was very strong against him. The days went very difficult for me too. Imbecilic sass talks among people in school and society kept me house arrest and Golu, he was strictly restricted by his mother. In between all the situations, Mom got married and Kartic uncle proved himself a good family man to us. In a way we found our lost happiness. Mom strongly believed that we are going to have a baby boy but Kartic uncle wanted a baby girl who has a pretty face like my mom. Whatever may be but they are happy together. Finally, the shadow of loneliness vanished from her life. Mom has become ecstatic and laurelled women again with a side effect; my bed time head massage was missing. Smita Aunty has a different opinion on our family. According to her, we are a family of thugs. We don't respect the value of culture and in reference of that she avoided us. She was not the only one many of the neighbouring families and colleagues did the same to Mom as to Kartic uncle. They knew teaching a blind society is foolishness so silence was the best answer they have. Tenth board exam was above the head and Raman was utterly busy saving his championship in Ray legacy game. Meanwhile, his grandfather spending each ounce of breath to fight against death daily. Like every day I was as usual packed my bag, buckle up my belt, and after kissing my baby brother's forehead run after the school bus. A lot of men and women were gathered near the Ray abate, crying, sobbing and among them Raman standing silently like a zombie. My curiosity tucks me there and saw dead body of grandpa in middle of the crowd. I was doomed. He was the last hope for me as well for Golu. Soon including my family a lot of others were arrived for funeral. People were coming and going, in the crowd my eyes were missing only one face and I understood where he was and to meet him must wait for moon to shine upon us. It was nearly twelve of night, dogs are barking and awls are lurking me as a prey, like a penchant I stopped near the backyard of Ray abet, exact below his room. Raman was unexpectedly waiting for me too. Holding a lantern in his hand looking at me like an awl. He had arranged a ladder already. I greened him and in return, he just smiled. I can see the pain in his eyes but controlled my emotion and climbed the stairs to him. He gave me his hand for support and pulled me into his room. We both are very close to each other for a moment. It felt like we both want to stay at that moment. All of a sudden a butterfly flew to Raman and seated on his nose. I laughed out loud but he put his hands on my mouth and whispered to maintain silence. I was conscious to the moment and he was focused on that butterfly. Before we can make any arrangements the butterfly flew away out of the window. It looked very beautiful.

Raman: "I'm sorry Akrit."

I looked at him silently.

Akriti: "Sorry for what?"

Raman: "I know the time is very tough on you and your family. You are being treated like a felony after that incident in school and then Kartic uncle and your mom..."

He got silent in the middle of it. I frowned, never imagined that Raman had that same thought too, and in anger, I was about to move...

Raman: "I have no means to harm your emotions, Akriti. I have no offense for it either; perhaps I'm happy for you that you got your family back on track."

Raman: "I'm sad because I don't have enough courage to stand with you in front of society."

Akriti: "That is not a problem Golu, I know very well your thoughts about me."

Our eyes mate for a moment.

Akriti: "And don't worry I'm always with you. Yes, your parents were not interested in the passion you wanted but trust me Golu they are not your enemy and you are not either. Don't let your willpower die."

He laughed out loud.

Raman: "Omg, Akriti you just talk like grandpa."

We got sad like grandpa left emptiness in our life, my heart was pumping louder, a sudden adrenalin rush and sole was yelling at me to speak my feelings for him but suddenly there was a knock on the door and we were distracted. It was his mom came to check on him, by that time I was safely hidden inside the bed. I can't listen what they talked but it was very short conversation. Thank God I was saved. That night we made a pact to look after each other like the old days. The tenth board exam was started and the days are happiest moments for us. Most of the time we spent together doing the group studies. Finally everything going as I expected, our love dots are linked. All these years we have been together as a friend but finally, we both realized that there was no need for any hide-and-seek game we had shared equal feelings and love the availability. We only worried about Smita aunty. The time was 3:00 noon the final bell rang and our exam was over. It was the English exam and I can see the satisfaction on the face of Raman. We both walked out of the exam hall at a time. A man was waiting for us and a police constable was with him. The constable stopped us and instructed to go principal office. A strange feeling of fear consumed us. We looked at each other and together walked to the Principal's office. The door was opened with a crunching sound and closed. That police officer again and principal ma'am was looking at both of us in worry. The day went and night has fallen on us, I was on the bed and the window was open. The sky looked deeply dark and few lightening stars. The last word of the policeman was still in my mind.

Policeman: "Arun managed to get the bail."

He only got bail not come back to school either to my life again and that thought helped me to get a good sleep. A shadow appeared from side of the window, gradually it stretched to the bed and its hand was touching my lips like enjoying it. I wake up and bite the hand in fear.

Raman: "Stop... stop Akriti this is me."

Akriti: "Golu!!!"

Akriti: "Why are you here in the middle of the night?"

Raman: "I think Akriti now I can see you fine and perfect so I must go and sleep comfortably."

He can't match his eyes to mine and about to walk away from bed. Before he could open the window I dragged him and grabbed in my arms, both of our eyes looked direct at each other like famished. Before his hands could protect him, I tuck the advantage and kissed his lips. He can't stop himself either, in a second we both involved like solely dreamed for this day. After fifteen minutes of the lips-locking game finally I let him breath.

Akriti: "I love that wildness in you Golu. It suits you."

Raman: "I don't know but finally I feel very easy and calm. Like a burden which I carried in my heart drifted."

Akriti: "Love you Golu, don't look me like that way... say it."

Raman: "Sorry, aaaa...... I love you and grateful that I have you."

Akriti: "That's correct my lovely duffer."

Saying that pushed him on the bed like 'finally time to hunt.'

***

A sudden sound of coughing forced the audience to get out of their daydreams. Slowly lights made the gallery fluently beautiful. She was still in pain and I have only option to feed her water. Thank God it worked; I tuck the book and mentioned the focus among audience. It was the last exam. The school bus was crowded and classmates were singing songs loudly and making promises to each other, exchanging phone numbers and tears. Many of my classmates were happy as well as jealous that I'm the only one who got the international exposer and going abroad for studies. But my eyes were continuously gone to Akriti, she was looking to me. There was a love bite on both of our lips and we both enjoyed remaining silence.

In middle of the crowd a group of girls were busy in a serious discussion.

Girl 1: "Ranee de is missing."

Girl 2: "Yes our super senior."

Girl 3: "Yes....yes got it. One of the most famous girls of our school and best part is...."

Girl 1: "Arun sir did bad things to her too."

Girl 3: "What do you mean?"

Girl 2: "You know...... what he did with Akriti."

The girl did say lowering her voice.

Girl 3: "You mean to say that there might be a chance Ranee de was tuck by Arun sir."

Girl 1: "Yes police convicted him and went to his house but due to the lack of evidence he was not arrested."

Girl 3: "This man is a master mind criminal."

I swallowed in fear and looked to Akriti. She was listening all these too.

The school bus stopped and we both alighted, Akriti was silence. There are a lot of unwilling thoughts were hitting her mind. I wanted to go with her but her mom and little brother arrived, I think this news already on TV. We exchanged smile and I walked back to home. I was about to hit the bell but door was already opened and in middle of the gape of the door I saw father was soughing on mom and they had a serious fight. I was confused and widely opened the door. Seeing me he stopped, collected his gears and left the home. Mom disappointed like guilt consumed her deeply. For the first time he was that furious on her. I thought not to trouble her and went to my room. It was 9:00 'O' clock and I was on bed. My eyes were tired but not found the right way to sleep. Continuously wiggled to the one side to another, worry eating me slowly like darkness. I can't live her behind when she needs the most. I felt suffocated and walked to the window and inhaled a deep breath. The sky looked free of burden in direction of cold moon light. Trees, grounds, roads and houses were looked so silence but are very dear to me. All of my childhood was spent around them. I do realize it because in a few days I am in another country, chasing new situations. A slight layer of tears in my eyes, I was missing my golden days with my grandfather. He was the only man who kept me think like a creative one but I think my child days are over now. I must have to move on which was practically not possible. With that question I gasped painfully and looked to sky. The early morning sunshine was smiling upon me. The day was very sunny and due to summer the sun was little dominant on Odisha. Akriti was on the roof helping her mother to prepare the mango pickles and her little brother was putting his best effort to disturb her. She looked to the stairs and dismayed, I think she didn't expect me and it was obvious we always mate in shadows of moonlight. Aunty got happy and the little prince was looked me with the humbling smile.

Anita: "Hello Raman!"

Raman: "Good morning aunty."

Anita: "Good morning.....very good morning."

Anita: "How are you and how are your preparations for Boston?"

The smile was faded.

Anita: "Wait here I will make you your favourite mango juice."

She went to the kitchen. Akriti remain like no one was there and busy in the preparing the pickles. I harrumphed, she gave a side look. I moved a little forward to her and touched her back. Something unique energy tickled my body, an attraction unexplainable.

Akriti: "What you are doing stop it."

I think she felt that same.

Akriti: "I can understand what is in your dirty mind."

She spoke with an interesting smile and kissed my cheek lovably. I can't match my eyes to her and a shy smile was on my lips. My face got red and she blasted in laughter.

Anita: "Why are you both giggling and Akriti you didn't finish yet."

Akriti: "Why are you in such a hurry mom, can't you see in a few days Raman will be away from us."

Anita: "Stop Akriti.... don't take it personally Golu, after all you are getting an opportunity to explore the world and learn the necessary survival instincts and trust me dear you deserve the opportunity and good news is your parents are capable to give you that."

Aunty told all that wisely and handed me the juice. Akriti can't tolerate the affection her mother has for me and looked frowned to both of us. We both laughed and looking to us she made the cry baby face. The summer vacation went well until the day of result. The night has passed and the day of judgement arrived. It was 11:00 'O' clock of morning I was seating at the main hall of the house and my mom was walking around me. Worry, tension, and fear was clearly reflected from her face. She was continuously looking to the wall clock and to my face then to the main door. A car was arrived and stopped near the door. Mom walked faster and mean while father was entered.

Raghab: "Stop there dear, have some patience."

Mom was worriedly looking to the calm and smiling face of him. Tears were at the edge of her eyes.

Raghab: "Don't worry dear your son topped the exam."

For a moment she has no expressions, stunned. Tears rolled out, breathing was tight and suddenly hurried towards me and hugged tightly. It was her proud moment.

Raman: "Mom it hurts."

I said funnily. Father was laughing looking both of us for a while and then came hugged us. There was a folded paper he was holding in his hand.

Raman: "Papa what is that paper."

Raghab: "Oo... thanks you remind me, its Akriti's result. Go and give it to her mother. They must be expecting."

Smita: "What are her numbers?"

Mom asked it in ego.

Raghab: "She did well, actually I never imagined it. She scored 72%."

He said it proudly. I tuck the folded paper from father's hands and walked to Akriti. I was happy and my steeps were jumping and dancing. Singing some Odia song and waving my hands like Mickle Jackson. The reason was Akriti. She performed beyond the expectation. In five minutes I was on her door steep and about to knock but the door was opened. Aunty was standing in front of it and she has the exact expression like my mother. I gave her the paper and looked into the house.

Anita: "I'm so sorry son come in."

Raman: "No problem aunty go ahead and see her result."

Speaking that in a mysterious way I entered to the house. Kartic uncle and Akriti was already seated on sofa. Seeing me at that moment she got a bit frowned.

Akriti: "Ooo.... topper."

She asked in jelousy.

Raman: "Yes looser."

I taunted her. A war was about to begin but suddenly her mom hugged her affectionately. Kartic uncle had come to see the results.

Kartic: "Waa..... I never expected Akriti can do that far better even the situations she has gone through."

Everyone was looking her in a proud expression but she was confused and snatched the piece of paper and saw the bottom line. Her eyes suddenly charmed gracefully and she looked direct to my face mesmerized, but happiness never stay longer as we expected so it happened to her. Aunty received a stress call from police station.

Kartic: "Who is it?"

Anita: "Police....."

Anita: "They said the girl who was missing found dead. The killer abused her a lot and after he reaches to his pick of the obsession he brutally destroyed the general parts of the girl and due to heavy bleeding the girl died."

Few drops of sweat followed to the chin and Kartic uncle swallowed in fear. His eyes were directly looking to us. Unknown to any of this situation we were busy in playing with the little baby. At that moment someone was knocking to the door, we all looked to that direction. Papa was standing there.

Raghab: "I hope I'm not disturbing you, by the way Akriti well done..... you did well..... No one ever expected it."

Her cheeks were glowing red and in shy she looked down.

Kartic: "Sir please comes in."

Raghab: "No kartic some other day I'm in hurry. Raman has few days to go, so his mother and I decided to spend our days with him as much as possible."

Kartic: "That's a great decision sir."

Raghab: "You looked little confused Kartis, everything okay!"

Kartic: "Yes of course sir...... everything is fine."

Kartic uncle ended the last word with a stress.

Raghab: "Sorry Akriti I have to take Raman away from you."

I smiled seeing papa happy.

Akriti: "No problem uncle he is all yours."

She said it so cutely but has a secret compartment in her heart which I only have access and it was clearly dark and sad. But I have no choice, my parents have very little time to spend with me and I have no rights to take away their feelings. The entire day mom was running after the cook and prepared beautiful dishes throw a party and invited her dear friends and their children. Some of them saw future son in law with in me which was way annoying. I knew neighbours are not allowed so it was difficult for me to stand behind mom and keep smiling but it was not for long. The front door was opened and someone entered very dearer to me.

Akriti: "Don't worry Golu I'm here with your mother's permission."

Totally ecstatic.

Akriti: "Why you are always such a looser and conjured of everything. Truly dear I'm worried who going to rescue you from troubles in that foreign land."

Pulling my leg was one of her hobbies.

Akriti: "Let's see tonight how brave you are!"

After ogling me daringly she gave a beautifully packed gift and left the place. The night was young and in time the guest numbers were reduced and finally the party was over. I was so tired giving fake expressions to the guests. All the energy of my body was drained and like limping I was dragging my body to the room and locked. I felt so drowsy and didn't realise how and when I went to the bed. It was almost 01:00 'O' clock I felt something tickling thing near my nose and sneezed. A slow and sweet smell of rose perfume and a very pleasant smell of shampoo forced to open my eyes but I delayed. Akriti was already locked her lips into mine and her tongue was started moving in my mouth. I didn't oppose and snagging her very romantically. Slowly she slides into the blanket; her body was tethered in tenderness. I moved my hands on her back slowly and steady to the down. She was wearing a silky night robe and her body shape was reflected through it. After a while we looked each for final permission. She removed her night robe, we were naked. I can see her beautiful body through the glimpses of the moon light. Her nipples were pointed. The situation was very different and difficult for both of us but we can't control and like a penchant I moved my hand on her softly. Akriti moved her hand into my body like I was her prey and slowly her hands were moved down between the leg. A different type of anxiousness on her face. The situation goes out of our hands and I ride upon her. She kept moaning until I go to the ideal moment. It was 6:00 'O' clock of the morning. Two small birds were intruded through the window and travelled around the room. Finally they were settled on a place above the bed. Their sweet sounds were forced me to open my eyes. I was smiling and my whole body was tired like all of my energy was drained away. With a sweet smile I looked behind. The bed was empty and I'm naked. For a moment it felt me like a figment but aroma of rose perfume conformed me of my sweet night. The happy smile was not for long on my lips. It was well understood she has done this because we are not going to have time for us after tonight. Mood was swinging like a tossing of coin. A moment the opportunity pushes me to explore a better world and other hand I'm scared of leaving my loved ones especially my newly discovered love, perhaps to my recent situation If I'm not going downstairs right now mom will barge into room which will not good for my love life. Like always papa involved in his newspapers, mom was serving the breakfast and marking my imbecilic unusual expressions like wanted to read them and I'm unknown of it sublimed in thoughts of Akriti. Doorbell rang?

Smita: "Dear what is that?"

A bit of anger in mom's voice.

Akriti: "Mother had prepared something for Raman."

Raghab: "Why don't you join us Akriti!"

Papa said delightfully. Akriti looked mom for a permission. My eyes were down on food. A momentary silence was on all of us face.

Smita: "Yes dear you are right it is after all last day and I don't want to upset Raman. Please join us Akriti."

Without a second thought she pulled the chair and seated next to me. Mom smiled out of jealousy but she managed to keep her anger silence for the day. Breakfast was extravagantly delicious.

Raghab: "I just have emergency works to figure. I promise you in a no time I will be at home."

Papa kissed my forehead and tucks the coat behind the chair and walked out. Mom was silence until the car gone away. Akriti and I were eating very slowly. We want to spend our time together but mom has different idea.

Smita: "I think Akriti you had done enough breakfast and of course I and Raman together like to enjoy the food your mother sends for us."

She nodded her head and pulled the chair slowly like she has no mood to go away from my site. Again our eyes were mat and she went away. All the day I was busy in attending VIP friends of my mother and of course her all friends were had a similarity and that was they all had daughters. The time was moved faster beyond my imagination. It was 3:00 'O' clock and humidity was at its height. I walked to room and shut the door, relaxed and wiggled. Akriti was already there seating near the study table. My eyes were widely opened in tension.

Raman: "What are you doing here.... did anyone saw you?"

Akriti: "What do you think Golu?"

There was a clear visible anger in her eyes. She tucks all the risk to spend the day with me and I was cowardly avoiding it.

Raman: "I'm sorry Akriti I have that exact intention but can't help it."

She listened to the end and immediately hugged me, we cried. All our life we pretend as friend, but when we learned the true pact of our relationship time and situation fucked us.

Raman: "Akriti...."

I tuck her to the bed and moved my head down between her legs slowly. I was out of control, in-fact she was enjoying leaking. When it was my turn the door has knocked.

Smita: "What are you doing dear, everything fine?"

Smita: "Are you eating something?"

Raman: "No mom of course not.....just drinking water."

Raman: "Why you are here?"

Smita: "Actually dear I'm here to introduce one of my very oldest friends might you know her, she and her daughter are here to visit you, wish you luck for your further studies. I think you must attend them."

An odd sound came from the direction of cupboard like laughter. Mom stubbornly looked around the room and walked to the cupboard, suspiciously wanted to open the door;

Raman: "Yes mom shall we go?"

She has looked me confused but attending guest was in her priority list so for the sake of God I was saved.

Akriti: "Wait me to the dawn Golu, I'm going to teach you another lesson of how to do unforgettable love."

Seeing that piece of note I smiled shy and jumped on the bed delightfully. But my happiness was perished with a gentle knock on the door. I put that piece of paper in my pocket and went to open it.

Raghab: "Hey buddy I have a gift for you!"

He was holding a beautiful jacket.

Raghab: "Are you busy son?"

Raman: "No papa."

Raghab: "Son you didn't pack your luggages yet!"

Raman: "Don't worry I will do it."

Raghab: "Sorry dear I'm nervous because I never send you out of my shadow, but I have to!"

We both seated on the bed close to each other, I thought this is the perfect moment to cancel this entire abroad concept.

Raman: "Papa I'm thinking why to do this? No one is going to be happy. Is it necessary to study in abroad?"

He looked melting.

Smita: "This is enough Golu, no excuses."

Raman: "Mom."

yelled.

Raghab: "Your mom is correct Golu, The privileges you are getting your classmates were only can dream about it."

Father said it with a wide smile and they both kissed my forehead.

Raghab: "And son tomorrow 4AM the train will be departing to Delhi and you will catch your flight for Boston there."

Raman: "Yes papa."

I replied with a pleasant smile. Finally I accepted my fait and packed luggage's for Boston. It tucks me four and half hour more and that restlessness bring me to the bed. Night has become romantic and younger like my love. The moon light entered through the open window, looked like sprinkle of silver dust. A shadow of women jumped by and crawling slowly with help of hands to the bed. It was full of dirt and pain. Stinks like a pungent smell of blood.

Raman: "Akriti.....!!!"

The dream conjured me and wakes me up like a freckle frog. I was hurried to the window, it looked usual, no tress of her coming. Akriti never did this before.

Raman: Is she okay?

Starting a new life at Boston:

Time moves so faster then a yellow line metro at Boston. It is now three years my days were very prolific and situation demands extra. I'm saying this intellectual way because my sole wants something and my mind want something and according to my current status my body act on different thing. Crossing the checkpoint I and my friends were entered to the metro. It was a little crowded then the usual day and that's because of a special occasion. We are finally graduated from Boston high school. In the compartment there were other office going people but the shouting, dancing and the way my classmates were showing the intention of freedom, it looks like whole metro was a classroom of mischievous students. Some of the old grumpy grannies looking us like a felony but my classmates are not bothered. I was seating in a corner enjoying the view, all of us wearing a black robe and the cap looking unique on our head. In the middle of it John my roommate and Rani an Indian American girl popped up for a group photo. They are the only family I have in Boston. It tucks me back my first day in Boston. Everything looked new and everyone was moving faster. I tuck out a snippet of paper from my jacket. It was an address written over there. I looked back to the luggage and then to me in the reflection of the automatic opening and closing door in front of me, gasped. I was on my own. Reflection of my dearest people appeared before my eyes. Smiling face of mom and papa. Loving moment with grandpa and the intimate moments with Akriti.

Raman: "What happened to her? Why she didn't show up in the last moment. Why I'm feeling the itch that something is wrong!"

In middle of that thoughtful moment a group of people pushed me out of the airport with them. I looked around. The city was crafted with European culture and the livelihoods are suggested with the Asian culture. I walked few steep out. There was a white car standing and a man of my father's age was looking for someone. He had a white board in his hand and my name was written on it.

Raman: "Are you looking for me sir?"

The wise man looked for a moment and then smiled.

Aman: "Aren't you recognizing dear I'm your Aman uncle. Oooo..... sorry you are only a baby by that time."

He gave me a thorough look and opened the gates of the car. He shared many stories and I can say he was very happy helping me. My focus was shifted from Aman uncle to the city. The city was as exact as I did read in books. Clean cobblestoned roads, European cultured infrastructure and modern Asian skyscraper's both are beautifully mismatched and the speciality of the never sleeping beauty of the city astonishing. Within a couple of hours we arrived to his home and the girl who opened the door for us was Rani.

Rani: "Hey wake up Raman we are at station."

My eyes were opened and felt dizziness like just arrived from the time travel. Within a few moments I was out from the metro and dissolved in the crowd of the Boston city. John and I were arrived to the apartment which was nearby Rani's house. I went to my room and fall on the bed. The time was already 6:00 pm. suddenly heard a noise from the drawing room. I was worried and in a hurry rush towards the direction. Rani was just arrived and John was shouting looking something in her hand. She gave a gentle hit to his forehead and walked to me.

Rani: "This is a parcel from your home and with it!"

It was an I-phone, Smartphone was a new concept for us and having an I-phone was too good.... it means totally cool. But my focus was on the letter.

Raghab: "Hey buddy congratulations, It is like yesterday you are out from your mother's womb and looking to the world full of chaos in amazement. You were a size of peanut and your little hands were playing with my fingers like toys. Look at you now dear. I'm proud of you who you are and now it is time to give you a professional shape so you can be more agile and lead your life precisely."

I put the letter on table and looked through the parcel. There was a folded paper inside the envelope. I tuck it and carefully opened. It was an application form of Boston school of law.

Rani: "So now your carrier is finally decided. Boston school of law."

I was confused and feared seeing the application form.

John: "Why don't you tell them Raman!"

Raman: "What should I tell them, that their son is a talented writer and story teller aimed to pursue his carrier in creative scopes? Its sounds like a fable. Isn't it!"

Rani: "Yup... you are absolutely correct Raman but fables are written by writers only. We are talking about writing and the profile of a writer because it has some extraordinary feelings for wellbeing of world."

What she said was good; I can say wise words but can't work with the real world. You have to earn grads, degrees which satisfy your salary and can get you a good married life and more over that a lifelong insecurity.

John: "Hey Raman your call!"

I got out of my thoughts and tuck the call.

Raman: "Hello...."

Smita: "Hello Golu mom is here beta."

Smita: "I hope I'm not disturbing you dear."

Raman: "No...No mom you never."

Smita: "Actually I thought that it is your first Smartphone and the first call should be from your mother!"

Raman: "Ha...ha..."

Smita: "Ha...ha...ha..."

I thought it was the perfect time to ask about Akriti.

Raman: "Mom I got the letters."

A silence like she was thinking.

Smita: "Yes dear I know that."

Smita: "I knew you are a talented mathematician but your father have plans for you."

Raman: "Yes mom practically."

Disagreement was clearly proportion in my voice but I had one choice to remain silence. The very next day morning John and I were going to the Boston law school. After changing two metros and walked a few steps in cobbled stoned beautiful road finally we were arrived to the gate of the college. The college was more like a castle.

John: "Wow is it a college...... I loved it."

John said in amazement and we both entered through the gate. A historic statue welcomed us. It tucks a day to visit the campus. By the noon of 06:30 we tuck the metro and within a few hours we are in front of house banging the calling bell. John was almost crossed the lines of his patience and about to push the bell once again 'surprise'. With that huge noise the door was opened. All of our classmates were standing and in front of them Rani holding a beautiful cake.

Raman: "Happy birthday John."

He looked me and then to the crowded gathering with his glowing eyes. John walked to the cake and cut a slice of it and put the whole big slice into the mouth of Rani. All of us were bust out of laugh. Rani, she was miserably grasping the cake. The event went well. Everyone enjoyed and all credit goes to Rani. She planned very perfectly, almost midnight few of our friends were left and few were not in a condition to walk. I was drunk and my dizzy eyes were searching John and Rani. They both are in the attic fucking brutally. It reminds of my days with Akriti. Truly she knew how to keep a man happy. The morning was a little hectic. I woke up in cold, breathing was steaming out and I coughed. All the night the window was opened and the room was surrounded with the fog. Everything looked blurred but somehow I managed to find the window and about to close, a blood smeared hand was caught my hand tightly and slowly pulling me out to the window. I woke up suddenly in hinder 'Akriti'.

John: "Good morning king of dreams, I herd a whisper a name Akriti, so came to check up on you."

Raman: "Yes, thanks for asking."

I said yawing.

Raman: "What all these John."

John: "You should appreciate me I brought you breakfast, where are your manners?"

He was well dressed and looked descent. The way he was talking I'm sure he needs something.

John: "Rani had decided to join the civil engineering."

Raman: "So..."

I said with a tricky smile. John got shy.

Raman: "Okay John I got it. But you have to realize that we need to submit our admission forms by today unless I don't know about you but my family is going to kill me."

John: "Ha...ha... yes dear friend precisely you are not ready at the moment and for your information Rani will join us. Her college is just a few steps ahead of ours."

The time was 10:30. The morning shines very fluently above the head along with the logo of Starbucks was blushing. I was seated at the outdoor. There was a beautiful bell hanging above the door of the café and it rang when someone enters through the doors like the old-school classic café. I was enjoyed the bell sound and an idea of amusement was intrigue me. I Started drink a sip of coffee with every ring of bell. Half an hour passed I was with second mug of coffee and the play time was gone. Only remain was frustration and anger. John was supposed to be with me but his curiosity remains with Rani. I knew we are going to be late and in middle of that thought the door was opened with the bell sound, a girl entered. I only can see her back side 'Akriti', no how she supposed to be here!

Instantly I walked to that direction but she was vanished out of thin air 'where did she go?'

Rani: "Raman.....Raman lets go."

John: "What are you looking for....Raman It's too late and we have to submit our forms, we only have a day."

Raman: "Guys you can carry on I will join you as soon as possible."

Like a lunatic I was looking each corner of the café, looking every face who is going and coming, people struggled of my imbecilic approach and finally few staff forced me to get out. I'm damn sure that was Akriti. John and Rani were in trouble too. They never saw me that chaos and forcefully tuck me out with them. All day long the memory of that café was hunting me. It was night 12:00 'O' clock. A very slow whispering sound was happened near my ears like a blow of cold wind. My eyes were opened and moving around. Slowly removed the white blanket and put my feats on floor. The floor was very cold, eyes were moved to the window. The white door screen was flapping to the direction of wind. I went to close the window, after all the cold at Boston was very costly for an Indian skin, but my eyes were stunned and mesmerized. The outside scenario was exactly looked like Odisha. Suddenly the white door curtains were stopped flapping and a ghost-silence was spread around the room. The moon light was getting dull. A very slow sound of scratching attracted my attention towards the study table. The vision was little blurred but I can feel a shadow was seating and scratching something on table, curiosity pushed me to there. The shadow was still involved in scratching, suddenly stopped and head was twisted, eyes were ice-cold.

Akriti: "Golu....."

That voice was very familiar, My hands were stopped and suddenly that shadow looked at me. I can clearly recognize those eyes. A glimpse of pain was reflecting from those eyes.

Raman: "Akriti..."

For a moment I was nervous but soon I gained control over my emotion and looked around, I was seating on my bed and the room was pleasantly silence. I tuck the water bottle from behind the table and juggled it to the bottom. The dream was mind-blowing. But the question which still hunt my sleep was why I was continuously seeing nightmares of Akriti, we had spent great deal of time together but I can't find our happy moments in my dreams.

Raman: "Is that so!"

Raman: "Is there everything Okay with Akrity?"

Raman: "Did she still love me?"

Raman: "Why she didn't call me?"

Raman: "Did she found someone else in her life!"

Raman: "Why she avoided me in all these years!"

Raman: "Why....why.....why?"

In frustration I did cry hollered and the silent midnight moon was the proof of my pain and a shadow which stand still behind the door until I fall into sleep. The night was full of hectic and the day was even worse. The noise of garbage truck awakes me. I woke in a dizzy mood. There was still a plenty of tiredness in my eyes.

Raman: "Oooo.... man not again."

John: "Don't worry Raman I did dump the garbage."

John entered to the room with two handful coffee mugs in his hand.

Raman: "It is magical bro. Without a dog fight my morning won't go well with you."

John giggling on my words and pushed his right hand to me. For a moment I looked him surprising and then tuck the coffee mug from his hand.

John: "It is life bro, unpredictable and unexpected."

Raman: "Never mind John, is it really you or a ghost of philosopher or may be poet."

I tuck the first sip of coffee and enjoyed the taste.

John: "Or may be a writer who stopped writing."

He completed the remain with a smile and tuck a sip of coffee. Suddenly I looked grimly to his face. There was firmness on his expressions. I understood John know all about the night.

John: "Bro I'm sorry I have no reason to trouble you but...."

He stopped for a moment like hesitated.

John: "Again you saw nightmare of Akriti and lost control on your emotions, right Raman."

I nodded my head like agreed.

John: "I saw a pattern in you."

Raman: "Pattern?"

John: "Yes Raman. Your love for literature is the only way which keep you stand and I saw the true happiness in you like you are blushing from inside to out."

Raman: "Stop that nonsense and be practical."

John: "I'm Practical Raman but are you?"

I was silent; my eyes were down and waiting to end the fishy situation. Sometime the direct truths are not easy to digest. John understood the unease and walked out from the room for sake of my comfort. I harrumphed and said...

Raman: "That day in that café I saw Akriti."

John: "What?"

He shouted and a curious happiness on his face. Soon he retrieved and seated next to me. Before his expectations were turned into anxiousness;

Raman: "I'm not sure that girl is Akriti but from the back she was looked exactly like that."

Now he realized it was my figment and gasped disappointed. He put his hand on my shoulder and said....

John: "Wake up bro there are plenty of girls around you who wanted to be friend with you, they want you truly for them. Find one and get rid of the nightmare of Akriti."

Saying that he walked to the door like a clever advisor, Rani was already there observing us.

Rani: "Oooo..... boys. You guys are so emotional."

Rani: "In a few days our lives are going to be change totally, and I want both of you behave yourself for the day."

John: "Babe what is today?"

Rani: "I knew John, Expected!"

She said grumpy and looked to my face but soon she understood that my expressions were resembled to John. She was very disappointed and walked to the downstairs to the main hall and we both followed her.

Rani: "Guys how you both could be so reckless. Today is our disco night. I rushed all the morning to arrange the tickets."

Her face was looked so innocent and we both were enjoined her childish behaviour.

John: "O...really."

John said very romantically and cuddled her softly. I harrumphed and they were both separated. I gave a gasp and went to my room so to leave them free to love. The window was open and a sweet smell of bread was soothing my nose. I went and looked out. The cars, bikes were everywhere. Few people walking coming and going for work, school and colleges. John always said it was my favourite spot and he was correct. I love to look the street, cobbled narrow lanes, café and the open shop which have the historic value. The window was a small

TV for me and all these people and their activity were like a live web series. Suddenly my eyes were stopped at a person. That was a she. Wearing a black hood jacket and standing behind a shop constantly looking to my window. Our eyes were mat for a second and she started walking slowly. Meanwhile I looked her stunned. It tucks a few more times to let me out of sudden shock and ran to the main door and opened it. Looked right to the left desperately. Those eyes are familiar, subconsciously walked to the middle of the road looking every possible shops and people around. If that was Akriti I don't want to miss the chance again. A sudden hilarious sound dragged my attention. A car was so close to me and any moment I was about to crush, suddenly a hand pulled and saved me from the Collision. I looked back, John was holding me terrific, darkness appeared before the eyes and I fall asleep. After half an hour my eyes were opened. I was laid on the couch. Rani and John both were seating surrounding me.

Rani: "Are you okay dear?"

I was looking both of them and because of dizziness my eyes were still fluctuating and those eyes hidden in hood jacket was still reflecting in my vision. I walk up lame and limping towards the main door and opened it. I saw everything was okay and the street was as usual crowded and shining. Following my unorthodox behaviour John follow me back to the house and set me on the bed like a mother taking care of her sick infant. Rani was silently following every situation. John looked her and understood she wants an explanation. It's true my eyes were closed but I can see through my ears.

Rani: "John what is it? He was again behaving like those strange panic attacks. I think he needs to continue his medication and the therapy."

John pushed her out of the room so I cannot be involved in their discussion.

John: "Stop those nonsense Rani, are you out of your mind. He is not a lunatic. He is a misunderstood genius."

He gave his strong preference to the last word.

Rani: "I know who he is and his creative sense. I want to save him from the nightmare of Akriti."

John: "I have an idea and need your help."

Rani doesn't believe him when he's talking about ideas but something was cooking in his mind which needs to know. They are gossiping something which was out of my reach but which I can listen was their tapping sound of shoes towards downstairs. An expression of confusion was carved on my sleepy face, but that has no use for the clock. The Boston city got alive again with another good morning and the reflection of cold sunlight was straight reflected on my face and as usual alarm clock was banging merciless. Yawing and with following meek twinkling sounds of birds eyes are opened and slide the blanket. I do sit for a while on the bed silently. A plenty of stuff running in my mind. It was my first day to the law school. I was excited as well as nervous. The tiny little birds were still poking the glass window and seeing them I thought we human are no different, giving continuous push is the only solution to bang the mortal world. In middle of the philosophy mood phone rang the iconic I-phone tune.

Raman: "Hello... good morning mom."

Smita: "Good night beta, I think you are just awake."

Raman: "I think it is night at India."

Smita: "It is midnight now."

Raman: "Where is papa, I want to listen his voice."

Smita: "By now you only can listen his snoring Golu."

We both laughed and immediately mom got silent like she wants to tell me something.

Smita: "It is your first day in Boston law school, Just remember dear, the privilege you have now others can dream only so don't waste it."

Raman: "Yes, Mom."

Ended the call with a faint heart. All these words felt like a heavy burden but to my condition I need inspiration and I know where to find it. After a shadow of doubt, a new energy of hope reclaimed and to find the conclusion of the day voyage to my new destination Boston School of Law. The climate and the college campus were properly soothing and its long history with the British colony intrigued. Almost looking like a replica of a British palace and from generations the institute served American soil as temple of knowledge and wisdom. Many of its students were served across globe with their unique approach and someday I will be one of them. My phone was blinked with a message...

John: Already stocking the bitches, keep it up you are in a perfect way.

At that moment few beautiful girls were crossed the way. I understood he was nearby and I turned around to look over.

Raman: "Where are you, bro....?"

John: Behind you. Boom....

I got scared, he was truly fast.

Raman: "Stop bothering me like a kid."

The classroom was different from my school. It was a half-circled big gallery and plenty of old-looking wooden benches and chairs were there. Many names were carved on them. The good news was we came earlier and chose an appropriate place in the middle row. It was a moment of enthusiasm for me but there are a few who never escape from their habits. John was already taking naps. I clicked a few pictures of him, evidence for Rani, and settled focused listening lectures. It was terrifically good for both of us. After the lunch bell there was a chaos between students like the old school, interesting.

John: "Why don't you wake me up?"

John said it yawing but his lazy whispering voice did not come to my ears. He looked at me I was looking around at the freshly new faces of the students.

John: "Raman...."

Raman: "Yes...."

John: "Are you looking for that mysterious girl?"

I looked frowned at John like my intention was caught. He smiled funnily and stood over.

John: "Come we should look outside."

The most beautiful feature of Boston college was its huge landscape and beautiful garden.

Rani: "I have been searching for you both all around the college."

John smiled at her and snatched the lunchbox like a child. She got frowned tucked it back forcefully and looked at both of us for an explanation. John was looking at me pitifully.

Raman: "Rani he is innocent and I'm the true reason."

She understood that I was searching for that mysterious girl. She seated near John and opened the lunchbox and gave it to him like a loving wife. He didn't waste a minute and ignoring her affection focused on food and started swallowing it all. I laughed out loud seeing the funny moment. There was a hidden sadness in my laugh and that reminds me of my school days with Akriti.

Rani: "Raman...Raman, where are you?"

Raman: "Yes, Rani...."

I replied to her after a moment like awake from a short daydream. She understood my condition and without complaining pushed a lunchbox to me. I tuck it and thank her with a smile. It won't tuck long to finish it but by that time these love birds were away for a good walk around the campus and the climate was way supportive. Suddenly a group of students were marching into one of the buildings and unintentionally my eyes were sticking to that bunch of crowds. It may be my luck I saw someone with familiar body language. My heart started beeping with unknown pain, my hands were sweaty, and automatically my legs were following the crowd into the building. It was art and literature building. The group of gathering ended up in a huge gallery and after me, the door was closed. I turned back but it was too late for me. I realized it was a welcome ceremony for newcomers and at the centre of the stage under the spotlight a middle-aged man was standing and looking silently and waiting for all to settle down. I was still standing near the entrance gate waiting for a perfect opportunity to open it. Suddenly the man looked into my eyes directly and harrumphed to say something.

Man: "Dear lad I think you are struggling to find a seat near a beautiful girl whom you can ask for coffee after the class."

The spotlight was now on me, I smiled jittery. Everyone laughed at me including the man standing on the stage. He raised his hand and the gallery was silent again.

Man: "Come son it is your lucky day, sharing the stage with me is a great honour for you as well as for your future..... Come."

The whole gallery was looking at me and I was looking at the man standing on the stage and giving me a greeting smile. I was walking towards the stage jittery and every step I was taking conjuring inside me like the Hell Gate was opened and I was forcefully pushed into it. In a few moments, I was standing behind him smiling at him as he does to me but my nervousness got kicked in when I saw houseful of fresh faces looking to me with expectation.

Man: "Thanks, young man. Now you are going to read a few paragraphs from this amazing novel and at the end, I'm showing you all the basic tricks that how you can become an influential reader and how you can pursue it as your profession."

After giving that long and graceful speech he left the stage and I was looking at him walk away like an idiot. The huge silent crowd was straight looking at me. I didn't even find a chance to elaborate. To hide my fear I was looking through the book cover and read the author's name.

Raman: "Leo Tolstoy."

Automatically a smile appeared on my lips like an old memory was turning its pages again in the present time. I heard a whisper of my grandfather......

Grandpa: "What are you waiting for, take a deep breath and realize the creativity engaged inside your heart."

I don't know what happened to me, suddenly a godly energy flowed into my body and automatically I started reading. I only felt that I was in my grandpa's library standing in front of him and reading fluently like it was my everyday job. The time limit they gave me was ten minutes but it was an hour still no one interrupted me to stop. Thank god finally, I came to my consciousness and stopped reading and looked to the audience. They still looked at me as motivated and expected, I looked at them confused. There was a momentary silence from both sides. A sound of clapping from front row and following that a plenty of many cracking of claps created positive vibes around the gallery. I was about to go, suddenly a hand stopped me behind. I turned; it was that man, looking at me respectfully like grandpa does.

Man: "Lad, what is your name?"

Raman: "Raman... sir."

Man: "Nice.... Indian!"

Raman: "Yes..."

Man: "There was another Raman whom we all known as Ramanujan... The greatest of all mathematicians and a visionary person beyond his time. When you are reading on stage I felt that exact for you."

I was silent, somehow managed my emotion, the clapping noise was still running around and the man was looking at me like a miracle. I can't tolerate the sudden happiness and left the auditorium. All the day I was seating in my class regretting of choosing a profession liked and resembled the societal statement not me. Those words that man said were hammering, corrupting my thoughts continuously which were painful to ignore. My heart was sobbing silently and pain was unexplainable, havocked in the thoughts of the past I opened the latches of the door. I saw throw everything placed as they should be. With an emptiness in my eyes, I gasped and through the bag on the couch. From the back John pushed me and I walked stumbled into the house.

John: "Wake up dream boy you are at home."

Rani vouched for me and hit his head.

John: "Auch..... Rani.......don't you dare."

Rani: "I already dared."

Rani: "Grow up and stop that childish nonsense."

John: "I will not give up."

Rani: "Then I will make you John."

John: "Try me... little princes."

Rani: "Don't call that name..... Or get ready for consequences."

John: "Oo.... little princes.....little princes.....little princes."

Both of them frowned and tucked the pillow from the couch, It was now a question of who was going to begin the fight but before that, a sound of door slamming, and they both stopped and looked upstairs.....

Rani: "What happened to him."

John: "How could I know?"

Rani: "You were all day long with him."

John: "I'm not his bodyguard Rani and you know well that staying upset is his daily habit."

She can't stop angry on him but the young girl had done enough for the day and tired, so it will be a righteous decision to take the matter on count for the next day.

***

The morning was as usual for me, sunlight was reflected on my face and finally after a couple of minutes my sleepiness was hatched. The expression on my face was robust and it deserved to be. John was standing near the window. I was looking at him like an angry bird.

John: "Bro it's seven don't you want to go for classes today."

I waved my head very childish and he laughed at it, slid down from the bed, and walked like a drunk to the washroom. John came to the doorstep and standing there in a relaxing posture looking at me brushing the teeth. I saw his reflection in the mirror and winked. He stood there silently looking at me. After a healthy tooth brushing and splashing the fresh water on my face, my expression changed and John saw that. I wiggled at him. He was still standing silently near the doorway. His behaviour became more and fishy like he wants to extract some information from me.

Raman: "What is it, John? Why are you acting like that weird?"

John: "Yes, it is. I'm asking that same of you."

Raman: "What do you mean?"

John: "Where have you been after lunch, 'yesterday'?'"

He said very specific to the word and gave a detective look too. I understood he had some sort of information and now he was making drama to listen everything from my site. My eyes were instantly removed from his face and looked down at the desk. I behaved like busy doing something but John was stupid and stubborn. My head was still down;

Raman: "I was at the art and literature auditorium."

John: "And... why?"

I gave a gasp and looked to his face like finally it was the moment for my confession.

Raman: "I saw that girl again and at that moment I felt like I should grab the opportunity which God has given me."

Raman: "She was with a couple of other students and.... "

John: "And...?"

John said curiously.

Raman: "I followed her but I don't know how I was trapped in the auditorium."

Saying that I was juggled a glass of water and in disappointment looked at John.

John: "Let me guess Raman. You were invited to the stage for a reading session and the charm of your creativity sprinkled around!"

Raman: "Yes, I suppose...!"

An enlightened expression of happiness appeared on his face. I was still looking at him like a lame, instantly he ran to my bed and tucked the phone. Silently I was following his childish expressions, now his hands stopped working;

John: "I think he was the person who welcomed you to the stage."

He was showing me the pictures eagerly.

Raman: "Yes."

John: "Raman, do you have any idea who is that?"

An expression of childish excitement was on his face.

Raman: "No...!"

I shrugged frivolously.

John: "Duffer, he is the dean."

Now there was something I had to worry about. I moved fingers between hairs and reclined back in my chair, really worried. There was a silent pose. I was recalling every incident of yesterday. John was still busy with phone. He was stopped and showed me my Facebook page. Within a night, there was 80 friend request including the dean.

Raman: "Fascinating!!!"

It was beyond my imagination and stood from my chair like a penchant and went to the washroom. Punched a few slashes of water on face and looked into the mirror. I can see the tension running in my mind. One side was my parent's ambition, another side was my passion welcoming me with open arms, and another side these huge appreciations confused me. Tuck a deep breath and tighten my emotions.

Raman: "Let's see what is going to happen to you Raman?"

I said it to my reflection in the mirror and walked out. The city, metro, and people were as usual but why I'm feeling that? Time has stopped. Everything was moving slowly, I could see the tiny changes, and feel them around me. Automatically I was following every expression of the situation. A daughter had a colourful candy in her hand and her little fingers were pulling her mother's hand to the toy stall near the train station, At the same time the policeman was walking around and his expression was very funny. Likewise, I was feeling thousands of people at the same time and an intrusion was uplifted in me. After a long time, my sleeping creativity was awakened. I felt like I was looking at everything and at the same time, I was looking nothing. A sudden gravitational pull brought me to the present and realized that I was standing in the middle of the metro and the people around me looking at the fishy expression on my face. Suddenly I was alarmed. The metro was slow down and a few office-going people were running to the exit door. I felt someone was keeping eye on me. Red hair, black eyebrows, and bold blue eyes were enough to motivate anyone to fall in love with her. Wearing a deep blue outfit on white skin looked stunning. Both of our eyes were mat at a point and she stood from her seat. John was marking everything.

Girl: "Are you Raman?"

John: "Yes, he is ma'am."

He answered on behalf of me. She looked at him and gave a gentle smile. I was stunned. It was a genuine reaction. If a hot and happening girl came and suddenly called you by your name, your eyes were wide open mouth too. The heart will pump faster than the Boston metro. Yes, I'm in that position.

Girl: "You are that guy who shared the stage with dean. 'Yesterday'."

She said something again but I was only looking at her beautiful lips and then my eyes went to her beautiful cleavage. I wanted to close my eyes but can't help it and I was not the only one. Suddenly someone hit harder to both of our heads. Rani was totally frowned. She looked like a lion looking to a prey. I feared but John was frightened.

John: "Babe!!!"

He said jittery

Rani: "You?"

She holds a good grip on his neck and dragged him with her.

John: "Babe!!! Rani... dear I can explain."

Rani: "You better John."

People in that compartment looking at them laughed, and some were filming them, but Rani had only one demand. A better explanation. I was looking at John like a poor thing and suddenly a sound of breaks. The metro was slow down, gates were opened, and a huge rush. I looked around to find that girl but she had already vanished. Suddenly something clicked in my mind and I was out on the platform. The station to Boston College has arrived. All the day I was thinking about the girl, her eyes and...

John: "I know you are thinking about that metro girl."

I looked at his jealous face and the pain in his eyes. It was too funny for me and lost control of my laughter, unaware but broke the silence of the gallery. The lecturer looked at me annoyed and about to speak but someone has knocked on the door at that right moment.

Girl 1: "Hello, class."

Girl 2: "I'm sorry to interrupt but like to enlighten you first years the college is throwing a welcoming Partee for you and wants to congratulate you legally for choosing this law school as your family."

Two girls were entered from the doorway to the dice. I felt energized. The girl next to the first one was familiar to me. Yes, it was my mystery girl. I recognize her shoes. I was very excited and before my temptation pushed me to do any nonsense...

John: "Bro, are you okay?"

He gave a weird look.

Raman: "Yeah...."

I controlled my freezing expressions and said in a jittery voice. But my true desire wants me to talk with the girl; I want to know more and more about her but the first thing I want to know her name. After that announcement, the class seemed to be very happy and soon the class was dismissed. John was happy; we got extra time to visit the college campus. Apart from the law school the Boston College was a huge place and collaborated with a variety of landscapes, gardens, and perfect outplace for creativity and love. Walking around the garden we went to the venue.

Several students and faculties were involved passionately in different dedicated jobs to make the welcome event remarkable. We found a place and settled. I was busy observing the activities of every tiny detail. John gave a side look and passed me the sandwich.

Girl 2: "Hello...."

A sweet voice dragged both of us toward the direction of the girl. My eyes immediately went to the shoes. Yes, it's her. I looked up, both of our eyes were mate, and glanced.

John: "Womanizer."

Whispered

Girl 2: "Sir..."

That girl said it in a loud voice. We both looked at her attentively.

Girl 2: "If you don't mind please find another place for lunch. We are here working for the welcome event."

I thought it was my golden opportunity to know her name.

Raman: "Thanks, I appreciate your Intention."

With a smile I was about to shake my hands, another muscular hand was moved around her shoulder. My graceful expression was suddenly stopped.

Tom: "Hey, Kathrin any trouble?"

Kathrin: "No, Tom everything fine."

Tom: "Can't you listen boys my sister doesn't want you guys here."

There was toughness in his voice but my breathing was normal now. I thought he was her boyfriend. John silently marked my expression.

Blondie girl: "Hey.... Raman."

Again that red-haired blondie girl. She came over and saw Tom; they both exchanged an expression like they know each other but Kathrin frowned.

Tom: "Hey sissi let's go."

He don't want drama so he escaped cleverly and that blond girl too. But Kathrin wasn't she wants me to see through her eyes, smiled and walks away.

John: "What was that Raman?"

I realized that John was looking at me like observing.

Raman: "What was what?"

I shrugged and retorted like nothing happened.

John: "She is Kathrin Norman and that boy with her was Tom Norman."

He said authoritative.

Raman: "You mean the Norman foundation!"

John: "Yes, Raman."

Norman was a big name in Boston. It's a privately owned law firm and played a major role in American politics. Some say the firm has a majority stake in the real-estate industry after the 2008 market crash. All of this

Wikipedia information running in front of my eyes. It's a dream of every lawyer to get employed by Normans.

John: "Raman tell me your father owned a reputed law firm in India right!"

Raman: "Yes."

John: "Now I can relate."

Raman: "What are you relating John?"

John: "That, you are a very ambitious and visionary man and Kathrin Norman is key to globalizing your father's business."

Raman: "Shut your nonsense."

I said grumpily and tuck a bite of sandwich. The day went very happily. After the book reading incident, I became a celebrity at Boston College. People were recognizing me everywhere, giving me a welcoming smile, and instantly my whole life was changed miraculously. The day went very fast like the dream and now I'm in front of my house, with an unusual jealous expression John was looking at my graceful lightening face. Yesterday he wants a better life for me and I suppose that granted by god. I gave him a teasing smile and about to open the latches but it was already opened, so spooky. He tucks the baseball bat behind of shoes rack and I was flashing light. It was so silent even we listen our walking sounds. We both saw a shadow and ready to attack, suddenly table lamp was lightened. We saw Rani was seating next to it.

Rani: "Why you both are attacking?"

She said it with a wicked expression.

John, Raman: "No, we are not!"

We said at once in confusion.

Rani: "You guys are so irresponsible."

She was so annoying. We regretted for not taking action when we had the chance.

John: "What we did?"

John said it arrogantly in a motive to suppress her. She looked at him confidently and stood from her place, now John was in trouble. Like a Bengal tiger, she walked to him and stood next to his shoulder. So pity for this pore man, he was nervous and tried to hide behind me.

Rani: "Tell me......"

Rani tucked a pose and looked at John intensely interrogating.

Rani: "Did you acquainted with that red-haired girl again?"

Her voice was thick and eyes were still on John.

John: "Yes...."

Rani: "I knew it John you freak libido!.... brief it, Raman."

John: "Yes brief it, Raman."

John repeated the last word in anger.

Raman: "Rani something misled you. We were having lunch, she came and after a small casual talk she left the place."

Rani: "I think you are missing something Raman He was lurking at her."

She said the last word in frustration and loudly.

Raman: "How do you know that John was lurking that girl?"

Her mouth was totally zipped.

John: "Rani.... Raman did ask you something!"

She looked John in pointed angry eyes and he tucked his steep back again. But that magic didn't work on me. I looked at her straight like want an answer.

Rani: "Kathrin told me."

Raman: "You mean Kathrin Norman!"

Rani: "Yes."

Raman: "But why Rani? What is the point of acquaintance?"

Rani: "She is a common friend."

Saying it slow she walked out from the house. John was following her desperately. I was standing stocked. That name gave me a tickling Goosebumps. It means a lot which can only feel. For the first time I was blushing, thank God John was not at the moment or he could kill me. That night was special, no more scary dreams and no more baffling at the middle of sleep. Unlike the time travel the other day morning sunlight travelling through the window reflected on my face and when I opened my eyes John was standing near the window laughing like the exact yesterday.

Raman: "Why are you nicking my morning sleep?

John: "You should thank me Raman I'm your lucky charm. And you should thank me that you can afford to see my handsome lucky face just before your eyes switch to the reality of the world."

Raman: "Stop your nonsense you wretched human."

I said it in drowsy outrage and forced my body to get out of bed.

John: "Lucky ideate."

John muttered. I stopped near the doors of the washroom and gave a grim look.

Raman: "What did you just say!"

John: "I have interesting news which may alarm you."

I was still looking him.

John: "Last night when I went to convince Rani in a flow of emotion she told me everything."

Raman: "Everything?"

John: "Yes, Raman everything...."

Raman: "I come to know that Kathrin Norman has sight on you."

I sat on the bed like an obedient listener and John tucked the chair next to him. He sipped a half glass of water and looked at my face like ready to confess.

John: "You are correct, that day when you followed your mystery girl and ended up in a reading session, she was there in middle of the crowd."

Raman: "Then!"

John: "You think the fire is from your side but my friend the fire is from both sides. I think now you should take your steps forward and fulfil nature's demand and drown in love again. I can feel the god's intention."

His voice was so orthodox and put me in a deep thought. Slowly closed eyes and trying to imagine her. There was confidence and clarity in the vision. After a long time, I can feel alive and tempted. Within three days, Boston College has changed me a lot. What is this strange feeling? Opened my eyes slowly and stood from the bed. I'm enjoying this openness and walked in front of the mirror and looked at my face like questioning myself whether I was worthy of Kathrin or not!

Raman: "Let's find the answer in the welcome event."

Saying that to myself I went to the washroom and closed the door. The day had arrived and from the morning my dearest friend John and Rani were busy preparing me like I was going to marry. From shirt to the bow tie to the choice of blazer Rani had spent a great time in the town jumping shop to another shop and John was a master collector of shoes. A single thing that was common in the chaotic situation was their excitement for me. Finally, we got an opportunity to settle at the nearest Starbucks for a short coffee break.

Raman: "Tell me we are going for the college welcome Partee but the way you guys are behaving, I'm thinking of a date."

They both looked at each other like almost caught.

Raman: "What you both were cooking in your mind?"

John: "We are planning to set you up with Kathrin."

It was an honest talk from John. I expected it.

Rani: "Do you think we take control of your life Raman?"

Raman: "No, perhaps you were the people who have unconditional interest for me. And about Kathrin Norman, yes, I have a little soft feeling for her but I'm not sure what it is."

John: "That's my boy. Don't worry Raman leave it to me I will voyage your love to its true destination."

The day went busy and in the evening I was standing near the gate of Boston College. The landscape was looking astonished. People were surrounded by all the places some were enjoying the drink, some were busy with the Buffy and a few love birds played a slow romantic dance with the rhythm of the music. Two hands were slowly thumped on my shoulder. On one side John popup and the other side Rani. They both behaved like they were determined to set me up with Kathrin.

Rani: "John I think I'm thinking what you are thinking!"

John: "Yes, we both are thinking of a good dance and it will help us to keep an eye on everyone."

Rani: "Not everyone John Kathrin Norman."

John: "Yes, Rani."

John tuck her hands very stylishly and they both walked to the middle of the floor, looked very funny and were in a determined mood so I liked not to disturb their love moment and to keep me busy I grabbed a glass of juice and walked around the venue, taking a good view of the arrangement.

Dean: "Genius are always left alone so as you."

Carrying a glass of wine walking to me. He had a significant narrative smile and I have only a smile to welcome him.

Raman: "Hello, Dean."

Dean: "Don't be bothered about that Raman. You can call me professor."

Raman: "Sir..."

Raman: "About that I'm not a genius."

Dean: "Why do you think that Raman?"

Raman: "Because I'm never alone."

Dean: "I think you are talking about them."

Professor pointed his finger towards John and Rani.

Dean: "Believe it or not that day on stage I saw an extraordinary creative man and a lonely heart."

He got my emotional nerve.

Dean: "I don't know what troubles you but, son it is not a good idea to escape from the greatest talent you have. Your creativity is a blessing and one day it will become your greatest strength. Believe it or not, you can't rid of it."

I was listening to him very carefully and meanwhile, my eyes were following the woman wearing a white dress rushing towards the garden.

Raman: "Excuse me, professor; I'm worried that I have to leave."

Dean: "yes, of course, Young man. Perhaps she is Kathrin Norman a bright student of literature and she might have a crush on you."

Giving a mysterious smile Dean left the place so I walked away. It was dark out in the garden but bright moonlight and street lamps were making the surrounding serine. I was looking all around. Suddenly wiggled to the back. At a distance near the pond, I felt disturbances in the bushes. Pretending the sound of the shoes I walked carefully. I saw two shadows doing something on a chair near the pond. I swallowed a bit in fear and got down. Crawled and hide behind the bushes. I saw a shadow sitting on the chair and another shadow was sitting on it and swivelling cautiously back and forth and back and forth. I crawled a little closer and now I could see a shadow of a woman sitting on a shadow that looked like a man and moving back and forth. I understood what it was. A smile tickled on my lips and suddenly faded 'If it was Kathrin then!' That question gave a sharp pain in my heart. For the final, I want to confirm who they are? From the opposite direction, a few clicks of lights were flashed. And in those few moments, I saw the red-haired girl was half naked sitting on a handsome man who was not wearing pants. There were a few more clicks of lights from the bushes and they both were separated from each other. In a hurry, they are wearing their clothes, and suddenly a girl wearing a white dress reveals herself out of the bushes. That body language was familiar to me.

Raman: "Kathrin Norman."

She has a camera in her hand and walking toward them bravely like caught red-handed. I was at a safe distance looking at the boy, he was walking toward Kathrin and after a discussion; the boy wanted the camera anyway and forcefully galloped towards her. Something happened in my heart. It was pumping rapidly, blood flowed faster than usual. My head was bursting out of pain and I jumped between them, holding the hands of the boy before they touched Kathrin and pushed him forcefully to the pond. Kathrin was looking at me with wide open eyes and without further delay; she held my hand and ran away from the place. I don't know when but I was enjoying her touch. She was holding my hand very tight and in her other hand was the camera. She threw the camera to the boy. Everything was running in front of me in slow motion. I was smiling foolishly without learning the seriousness. I only can see Kathrin holding my hand and we both are running together. After a long time my heart was tickling again for someone and this time I made up my mind to fall in love without a second thought. And God permitted me. A deep desired rain and Kathrin was running in it tirelessly. At a point, she stopped in the middle of the ground. I can see very clearly raindrops falling from her head and going in between the cleavage.

Kathrin: "What are you looking at?"

Raman: "Beautiful.....no...no...nothing at all Kathrin!"

My eyes were still stocked at her bosoms and she noticed. She felt a little hesitant but I can't help it. The white dress was rinsed and I could easily look permeable into her clothes. I didn't want to ruin my first impression so I stopped lurking and gave her my blazer. She tucks it immediately and wears it like she needs it.

Raman: "I think the rain will not stop but...."

Kathrin: "But..."

Kathrin repeated my words and we both laughed.

Raman: "My apartment is nearby you can change your clothes there. Don't take my words other way I'm just a helping hand."

Kathrin: "Yes, you are right Mr...."

Raman: "Raman."

I retorted the last word instantly, gave a smile and she smiled back shyly.

After a few times, we were in the metro. Water was drizzling from our hair, the cloth was all rinsed and our lips were tethering in cold. Although the metro was not crowded our situation was perfect to grab the attention. Kathrin made all possible attempts to stay inside the blazer. We both gave a jittery smile to each other and found a place to sit. I was marking an old lady staring at kathrin constantly which disturbs her and she moved closer to me. I thought it was an indication of god and tucked her into my arms immediately. She didn't resist and settling comfortably. All that time I did feel her heartbeat as she does. It was like we sublimed in each other's body. Station has arrived and the old lady stood from her place and walked cautiously to us. We are looking at her carefully. She gave a thoughtful look from top to bottom, and opened her wallet. She offered money like helping us. Kathrin was astonishingly looking at that old lady and then at the dollars in her hand. We were way troubled and now no need more in that situation. She tucks the money and the old lady walked away waving a good luck smile to us. We are the last to walk out from the metro station. It was still raining and the blowing wind made it more maniacal.

Raman: "Don't worry Kathrin we are not far from my apartment."

My soothing words comforted her and with a smiling expression she held my arms and we followed ahead in the direction of the apartment. Because of heavy rain light was out and darkness kept us closer. The hiccups of the lightning thunder kept the street visible and we managed to arrive at the apartment. After a struggle in dark I made through the door and unlocked. It was difficult to walk around with dirt it could make it worst but let me tell you we are all in water. I clicked the switches twice but they are not working. Rain was out bursting crazily. I think the nature was too much happy like me. A very slow sound like something was dropped on floor and I wiggled. The blazer was already on the floor, meanwhile a ballistic thunder was cracked above the sky and the lights were reflected through the window. I saw her white wet dress looked like another layer of soft skin on her body. I saw almost a beautiful bikini body. Tenderness pushes my legs slowly forward to her. A maniacal ecstatic feeling coaxed me to walk close to her. Blood was flowing faster than bullet in veins and an unorthodox intention made me more powerful to push my feelings on her. She was not avoiding stand still like waiting for me to take the first attempt. A mixed feeling of fear and excitement tickled my heart, I was so close to her almost a distance of a finger. We both can feel the warmness for each other; only need a situation to prod us together. And it happened. I saw water drops falling from the head and slowly sublime in between her cleavage. This time she neither hesitated nor stopped me. The opposite happened. Slowly she tucks my right hand and put it on her bosoms softly. She doesn't have to put the same effort on my left hand. It automatically went there. My hands were feeling warm soft flesh and that feeling gave a sudden shock to the body. I can feel change in action. My hands were moving slowly on her bosoms and then on her whole body. Soon after we went to bed, our naked body was covered with a smooth blanket. She was making sizzling slow noises and I was on her moving back and forth, unstoppable.

***

Back to the present time the auditorium light was once again glowing brighter, Seems time was up. To the instant my eyes were can't resist the reflection but after a few moment everything fine. I can see a bunch of densely populated audience clapping and soughing. It seems they are emotionally touched with my romantic explanations. I looked behind, Akriti was looking at me. I waved my eyebrows for a reason, why? She waved her head like no. I smiled to her and stood from my seat and buckle up the blazer. She stood slowly with help of her support steak and joined me. I realized she was smiling to audience but there was no happiness, is she worried about Kathrin..... no I think perhaps not. She has some other reasons. I gasped and out from the deep thought. We both waved hands to the crowd gave autograph and selfies and while walking among them I saw a beautiful dressed woman was standing in middle of crowd looking constantly to me without any movement.

Raman: "Kathrin....."

Muttered.

It felt like eating a sweet poison, everything numbed, in that heavy crowd I felt lonely and frightened and like a lunatic ran towards the car. Akriti saw it; she was so happy seeing her but can't help it. Following me she entered to the back seat.

Raman: "Driver move it faster."

Akriti was looking at my face freaking out and the car was totally silenced until we get to our apartment. All the way I was looking outside the window, eyes are red and slightly moist. Like a time machine my past happy days with Kathrin was flashing in front of my eyes. After a pleasant bell the lift door was opened and we were walking to the apartment. A slow sound and the door latches are opened. The house felt like an empty place, there is no sole in it. I helped her walk carefully to bedroom. She was silence and observing every expression of my face and waiting for the correct moment.

Raman: "I'm going to bring some water for you, do you need anything more?"

Akriti: "Yes.... Raman."

Akriti: "An explanation."

I stopped for a second and about to walk away.

Akriti: "You think walking away is a solution!"

My feet stopped but I don't have that courage to wiggle and see through her eyes.

Akriti: "She was Kathrin correct!"

Raman: "Yes..."

I said in melancholy.

Akriti: "She was there for you and you.... ignored her like that?"

Raman: "Yes I ignored her just like that."

Akriti looked to me thorough and set her support stick to stand. Tuck a deep breath and collected the remaining energy in her heart and walked to me. She was looking like eighty year old women in a twenty-seven year old body. I turned and looked at her eyes. A clear agony, I'm damn sure if she was the old Akriti then my balls were already in her hands, but she was not. I saw her calm down and looked me kindly.

Akriti: "What are you doing Raman?"

Raman: "What am I done?"

Akriti: "Where are your manners? She travelled all along and you....."

Akriti: "All these years I was thinking it was my fault but now I can realize it was you who ignored me, the consequences I did suffer you are solely responsible for all."

She spat at me wayward.

I stand still listening everything she was throwing at me. Agony and melancholy filled my eyes with tears. My lips were shaking but if I do the dog barking then it might go wrong for her. She was breathing tired and seated on the bed slowly. I sat down next to her, after a silence she prodded the support stick to my leg and I kicked. The stick fall on the floor with a sound and we both laughed at once. I lunged at her gently and hugged affectionately.

Akriti: "Au...ouch...ou."

She sought in pain.

Raman: "Ouuu..... I'm sorry Akriti, sometimes I forget that you are not my old Akriti anymore."

Akriti: "Nither I could be Raman."

Raman: "Don't say that it hurts me."

Akriti: "Whether you agree or not my fate is decided, death is my ultimate saturation."

Raman: "Akriti you are alive and nothing is going to happen."

Akriti: "Don't chase after figment dear, it only gives you pain and loneliness."

I understood the hidden message inside the deep talk, moved closer, and grabbed her hands. She looked at me with a comfortable smile and clueless eyes.

Raman: "Akriti please try to understand Kathrin deserves better."

Akriti: "And no man is better than you Raman."

Raman: "How could you be so sure!"

Akriti: "Because I'm a girl."

Raman: "I left her in the middle of nowhere, unnoticed. Just like that."

Akriti: "So what Raman?"

Raman: "I'm a felony and deserve punishment."

Saying that I walked away. There was guilt in my eyes but Akriti was worried about the foolishness and put a hand on her forehead in worry. The night won't go well. Sleepiness was away from my eyes, it was maybe the 19th time I had wiggled. Next to me Akriti was sleeping, a satisfied smile on her lips. I could see outside the window the drizzling raindrops were banging and my thoughts were connected to the past again. Eyes are opened in sudden thrill. The mild morning light was covered inside the clouds like I was covered inside the blanket, all naked. Next to me, Kathrin was sleeping and a satisfied smile was on her lips. Slowly I slid the blanket and carefully wear the trousers. The breakfast table at downstairs were quit occupied.

John: "What is it...?"

Raman: "What....John?"

John: "I asked u first Rameeee?"

Rani: "Now if you both spat again, let me be clear I'm going to smash both of your heads and make a spicy egg fry out of it."

She sought out loud.

John: "Not bad Rani."

Bad luck for John. He won't take it seriously but the way Rani looked at him, if he dared to speak the next word it might be his last day on earth. I understood she won't need to be interrupted and I tucked the juice jar silently and busy pouring it into my glass. She tucked a slice of bread and ate like a hungry shark. John was still silent and waiting for her green signal. In the middle of that, we heard a walking sound downstairs. Both of them were looking in that direction in amazement.

Rani, John: "Kathrin...."

They both said at once. She was wearing my white long shirt. Covering her knees uncomfortably walks to us and silently stood behind Rani.

Rani: "Please have a seat Kathrin we just started."

John was still looking at both of us and trying to read our expressions. Rani was in her way attempting the best effort to comfort her. Momentarily both of our eyes were mate hesitantly. The game of hide and seek was continued until the doorbell rang.

Rani: "Coming!"

Two well-dressed bodyguards were waiting out. Rani stood stuck and saw them like a new species recently out of the zoo.

Lee: "Good morning dear I'm Mrs.Lee."

Rani: "Good morning I'm Rani.... how can I help you?"

She was still in amazement. The middle-aged Chinese-American lady walked close to the door and tried to look into the house.

Lee: "Dear, I'm looking for Kathrin Norman!"

Rani: "And what is your purpose to visit her?"

Rani retorted her rudely. Looking to her face the lady smiled gently and showed her phone screen.

Lee: "I was tracking the GPS since morning and she is at your home."

Kathrin: "Lee...."

A voice from the house. Kathrin walked to the door and hugged the lady. The way they are talking it looked like a motherly relation.

Lee: "Good lord, where are your dresses?"

A guard ran to the car and fetched a long black winter jacket. Kathrin wore and wiggled. Following her expression Lee looked into the house. I was there sitting at my place and looking at her with a desire for love, and after a goodbye she left. Lee was looking at everything like scanning our expressions. All of it happened in an instant; Rani couldn't figure it out and closed the door in slow motion.

Rani: "where is John?"

A fear induced on my face and I ran upstairs. The room door was opened and detective John was already on duty. Kathrin's white dress was in his hand and sitting on my bed he was imagining the scenario. The situation was out of my hands, like a cry-baby I stood at the doorway and looked at his evil face with the intention of fight.

Raman: "Back off John."

John: "It is her dress right!"

He showed me with a cunt smile. The Tom & Jerry fight has begun and in a few moments, the whole house is upside down. Someone needed to put it to an end so I lunged before he could run out of the room. We together smashed on the floor and finally, I clutched one end of the dress and pulled. The dress was torn apart like a white paper. The friendly sport ended up in a shrieking silence.

John: "Raman...I have no intention to...."

He was nervous and before he concluded his apology I left the room. Rani was at the doorway staring at us like she knew the conclusion from the beginning. She thought that it was the usual fight as we do but it wasn't. The last time was the day of the incident we ate together. Almost a week an unknown silence tucks part in our friendship. Most of the time I spend at outdoors of Kathrin's classes with a perfectly packed gift in hand but now the gift pack looks pail and it was asking me when you are going to deliver me. I began to think it was my foolishness to expect love from one nightstand, it was a Saturday evening after college I spent my loneliness with a delicious burger in garden near my house. I saw a beautiful black Mercedes come by and a lady alighted from it that was more elegant than the car.

Raman: "Kathrin...."

I muttered. The same old Chinese caretaker was with her. She said something to that old lady and followed her steps towards me. I can feel the essence of love again. She came by and seated next to me. I was excited inside but looked calm from the outside. She gave a thorough look from top to bottom and gasped relaxed.

Kathrin: "Where is my gift?"

Raman: "Where is what?"

I asked jittery and looked her nervously. She was looking at me with a narrative guile expression on her face and hit gently to my shoulder.

Kathrin: "Don't fool me, Raman, okay tell me if I'm wrong why you are waiting out my classroom every day with a gift in your hand."

Kathrin: "Whole college knows it for whom you are waiting and the......"

Raman: "Yes you are correct the gift was for you Kathrin but now it's no more."

She got tensed and the clever smile on her face faded away.

Kathrin: "You can't do this to me, Raman."

Raman: "What I did to you, Kathrin?"

Said it coldblooded.

She was truly dispirit for me and a few drops of tears gave me all answers. She was sad and about to go but found a touch on her shoulder. She turned. I was crouched and the gift pack was in my hand.

Raman: "Do you love me as I do Kathrin?"

Kathrin: "Yesss..."

She said it like a cry-baby and hugged me so tight. At a distance near the car, Lee was happily seeing both of us. She tucks us to a very old Italian restaurant of the town.

Raman: "So you do love Italian?"

Kathrin: "No....not so fond of but my mom does."

Raman: "Where is she, I never saw her with you?"

Kathrin: "She is no more...."

Raman: "I'm sorry Kathrin, my words are harmless. I have no idea about it."

Kathrin: "I know that Raman."

She moved her hand and tangled her fingers into mine softly.

Raman: "What are you doing?"

I shied and about to remove but she held my hand tighter. I can feel her feelings for me are so real.

Kathrin: "I suppose we are a couple."

Raman: "Yes... Kathrin."

Said it authoritatively.

Raman: "But we are here for a date right."

Kathrin: "Raman date is for hook-ups, we are lovers."

Raman: "Yes dear calm down, I'm well aware of it."

We laughed.

Kathrin: "Yes..... you better."

She said like showing her ownership on me. I smiled at her childishness and let the conversation continue.

Kathrin: "So where I'm!"

Raman: "At your mother."

Kathrin: "Yes...."

Kathrin: "She was an Italian beautiful lady and the love of my father. I have a lot of old memory with this place. It's her favourite."

Kathrin: "I remember we used to spend a lot of time here. Yeah..... she love to suggest the cook about foods."

Kathrin: "She was a very amazing cook. I remember how father used to praise her cooking talent."

She went silent and dived into her thoughts.

Raman: "What happened?"

Kathrin: "I'm sorry Raman."

She was emotional. I understood her rough patches and decided better not to scratch them.

Kathrin: "What we should eat then!"

Raman: "I'm telling you I have no idea about Italian foods."

In the middle of the talk, a waiter came and gave us fresh juices and left. It felt different.

Raman: "Kathrin...."

Kathrin: "Yup.."

Raman: "Tell me.... the place, is it owned by your family?"

Kathrin: "Yes, how you know?"

Raman: "Thought so."

In a few time foods served our plates. They are garnished beautifully and wait to chew up, but destiny has a different decision for us. Someone was putting his cunt eyes on our table. In the middle of giggles and laughter suddenly Kathrin goes stunned. Her eyes were following my back.

Kathrin: "Raman...I think we should go."

Raman: "Why we just started. Look at these foods I don't want to in-vain people's effort."

Kathrin: "Try to understand Raman the time is inappropriate for your food analysis."

Suddenly her face went numb. Her eyes are conjured and a hand swiftly touches my shoulder. I wiggled;

Raman: "Tom...."

Before I could say 'hey' my face resisted a huge punch, smashed on the table, food was all over me and I wake up. In dizziness, I was looking around for a confirmation. I saw the bed was empty and time was seven of morning. I pushed the blanket and saw a tray and two tea cups scattered on the floor and Akriti fainted behind it. I felt like my whole world gone. Immediately she was admitted to the hospital. I was sitting out on a bench. The doctor and staff were going and coming out of the room. After an hour Dr.Dev came and seated next to me. I was looking at him like a stupid. He put his hand on my shoulder like an older brother; Dr.Dev: "I'm aware the story session is important for both of you.... stage is calling her but..."

Raman: "But?"

I asked in worry.

Dr.Dev: "Death is on the way waiting for her. It is not the time to push her strength and you are well aware of it Raman."

Raman: "Yes, doctor you are correct. I will postpone the storytelling session until she catches her breath again."

Dr.Dev: "No Raman you are not getting my point."

I looked at him in a way trying to understand his point of view.

Dr.Dev: "She is permanent to bed now."

Raman: "Okay.....I will cancel all events."

Dr.Dev: "NO, you won't. If that is so then depression will kill her faster than the cancer."

Raman: "Then tell me doctor what I can do?"

Dr.Dev: "She has a request. A lady named Kathrin will continue the session on behalf of her."

Raman: "It is impossible."

Dr.Dev: "You have to Raman....you have to obey her last wish."

It was impossible how I can sit next to a girl whom I betrayed, left her alone for my own good. I went to the room and saw Akriti lying on the bed and a pipe went through her mouth. The ECG machine was beeping and I could see the desperate movement of lifelines on screen.

Finally, I was on the stage and the gallery was full of cheer and claps. The lighting and the music was cloying and I am waiting for her confident outside but totally nervous inside. Immediately the focus went to the entranceway. A beautiful-looking woman was walking on the red carpet to the stage. I was stunned; Kathrin was wearing the dress that I gifted her. My heart was pumping louder and emotion was so on to her. She was looking beyond expectation. Suddenly a bell rang in my mind and I was cautious.

Raman: "Welcome Kathrin."

Kathrin: "You too Raman."

She was looking atomic and the centre of attraction. Confident, bold, and stunning these three words narrate her body language appropriately. Without further delay, she tucked the book and moved to the next page.

Back in Odisha:

The night was so young and the moon was shining at my window. The feeling of losing someone precious kills me deep down. 'I hope Golu feels the same as I do.'

Akriti: "No I can't do it; I'm no saint and can't let my love go away."

Lying on the bed I was thinking, and suddenly wiggled to the other side. The moon was looking at me cutely and trying to convince me. Seeing it a lot of sass thoughts cooked in my little seventeen year old head.

Akriti: "No....it is wrong. I suppose not to become the villain of his life...yes how stupid I am."

Akriti: "If he finds someone else out there..... So.... what else do I do? No.... my Golu is not a swindler."

Akriti: "I should drop thinking this!"

Akriti: "Long distance relations are not working? Idea! He should pledge to marry me before the goodbye kiss."

Akriti: "Akriti aren't you over thinking.....hmmmmm."

In frustration, I covered my head inside blanket. Truthfully the self-talk flustered me. I turned and looked out of the blanket like a turtle head to the wall clock. The time was eleven; eyes went down slowly and closed. Meanwhile, a shadow appeared from the direction of the window and it looked wild and stretched towards the bed, someone walking close to the bed slowly slid into the blanket. I was smiling mischievous. A hand slowly touched my body and I was comfortable I knew it was Golu. But suddenly that soft touch became harder and painful.

Akriti: "Golu, what are you doing? It hurt me please..... please..."

Akriti: "Golu!"

Immediately I wiggled and soughed. Jolted a slap and realized it was not him. For confirmation I touched the face, it was rough and hairy, body stinks badly. My immediate reaction was to escape from the bed and go to a safe distance. Lips are tethering and eyes are conjured. Now the shadow slowly stood upon the bed and the blanket was removed. It was dusty but in moonlight the face was visible.

Akriti: "Arun sir....!"

whispered.

***

It was a small room. Walls are paled, blood stain on floor and in few places scratches. A dim light was above the head which was blinking. A pungent smell of medicine forced me to wake-up. I'm still in delirium; the last thing I remember was the ogre look of Arun sir. Someone started coughing. I was worried and tried to unlock but my hands are tied in chain. Helplessly looked to that direction and swallowed a bit in fear. It was moving. A girl of nearly my age came out from the dark. She was all dirt, wounded and groggy. It seems I was not the only prey for the libido maniac basted.

Girl: "Do you want water?"

She looked tired. I waved my head slowly and tuck the plastic bottle. Opened the cap and about to drink but it stinks like urine. Immediately I threw it away. Before I could bounce back she started crying. She was in deep trouble. The dress she was wearing was ruptured from many places, dark circles below the eyes, bruises all around the body, lips are turned white and looked like was not eaten food from many days. A sound from the outside of the room.

Girl: "Hide yourself he is coming.....he is coming."

Fear embodied in her deeply. I closed my eyes and the door was opened. That stinking smells again. Someone walked close enough and gave a thorough look on my body, and then it went to that girl and threw food on the floor. She was waiting until the door to be closed and jumped on the food like an animal. I was looking stunned. She stopped for a second and looked at me. My bailey was aching, our eyes mate and she threw some bread out of her foods. They are all dirt and looked awful. I was angry and feared at that same time, I never did wrong to anyone never, why me then? How I suppose to react to that girl and how I can deal with the rapist maniac, I'm only seventeen. A lot of things are running in my mind, disgraced and in worry looked around, few lights were reflected from a broken window, and it brought all daylight. Tears rolled out of my eyes 'Golu must have gone'. I cried out like a broken shit.

Girl: "Stop that noise, what are you doing girl?"

She came over and put hands on my mouth. I felt suffocated but she had a reason and the latches were opened. We hugged each other tightly and looked to that direction.

Arun: "Hellooo......hello.....hello."

Arun: "What you guys doing.....the lesbian stuff!"

Arun: "If you were planning for an escape, please it is only your figment."

Arun: "And...my dear love Akriti do you remember me or my touch will remind everything you did to me."

Arun: "Never mind where is your boyfriend. What is his name.....aaaaaa yes Raman."

Arun: "Oooo so pity he must be of travelling by now, America."

Arun: "So unfair with you, hmmm.... it is your rights to have intercourse with him for the last time."

Arun: "Don't worry daddy is here. I will keep you warm."

Akriti: "You will regret it Arun, pathetic piece of shit."

Arun: "Okay then you had your play, it is time to take off your pants Akriti...ha...ha...ha."

I can feel my nerves, heart was pounding harsh and sudden dizziness appeared before eyes. When I come to my senses everything was silence, room was empty only sizzling sound of breathing was with me. Someone was crying hollered outside the door. I rushed to the metal door and trying to listen. It was that girl 'what else that monster doing with her.' Luckily I found a whole. The situation was straight in front of me. The girl was on the bed naked, helpless and Arun was on her brutally raping. A monstrous smile on his face. After fifteen minutes the door was opened and the girl came to the room limping. I felt sympathetic and hugged her tight. She has no expression, like a living dead walked to her place and dissolved in darkness; it seems she has compromised with the situation. Meanwhile police search party was alert all over the Odisha. It was for first time a high-profile rape and serial killing case grab the attention of media and country. There are question on social justice, judicial capacity and clear negligence of police. In between public protest and political pressure the case bean handover to crime branch and my family, they are a fragile piece of an unsolvable puzzle. Brother was too young to understand the situation going on with his sister, mother already lost her focus on motive of survival in absence of me and Kartic uncle was keep busy in collecting the broken pieces of our family. The door was opened once again; he was appearing more like a predator. I swallowed a bit in fear because his hunting eyes are looking me more than a minute. The girl behind me was silent like she knew what is going to happen next. He lunged towards us like a hungry libido and catches the girl by her hair. She sought in pain but Arun was enjoying, leaking tongue like she was a delicious food to him. He gave a side look to tell me that next was me and forcefully tuck her out. I did pee in fear and cried out loud. A while after collected all strength together and walked to the door, tried to see through the whole but there was no one on the bed. Suddenly the door was opened and I was seating near;

Arun: "Mis.Akriti if you are done with eavesdropping I have few tasks for you."

He coaxed me to clean the kitchen and walked out like a gentleman. I felt safe and gave a look into the room. It was big, available with survival gadgets. Two single bed, one seating place attached with kitchen and a bathroom. The door of that dark room was near the bed. While cleaning the crockery's found a knife, I looked it cunningly.

Girl: "It is going to be dumb decision if you are thinking to get the knife, he is so clever."

I looked back, the girl walked close to me.

Girl: "There was another girl with me and one day she tucks a screwdriver and before she could create an impact he blew her vagina."

Girl: "It is still, like only yesterday happened, blood was everywhere floor, wall, roof, body matters are all on floor. Every day, I saw that in my nightmares, her genitals blow up like a balloon."

Like a good girl I put the knife at its exact place.

Akriti: "Hi....I'm Akriti. And...."

Namrata: "Namrata.... Namrata das."

We gave a faded smile to each other and involved in household works.

The day went better, kitchen was all set I helped Namrata to set the bed and finally the drawing room was arranged to call it a house.

Akriti: "Namrata.... truly you will become a proud homemaker."

Namrata: "I don't think so."

Namrata: "There is an invisible line between the figment and dreams. And we suppose to learn them according to the jeopardy we are in."

Namrata: "I don't mean to upset you Akriti but the reality is we are done, suppose we succeed to escape this place but this conservative society never welcomes us as we were."

She has a strong point and now I learned why she submitted herself to a psychopath like Arun. We got busy chopping the vegetables and involved in preparing the dinner. My attention went to a slow sound which was coming from the direction of the bathroom.

Akriti: "Namrata tell me do you ever try to see the things outside the room."

Namrata: "No he never permitted me to go out of this room."

Akriti: "He...."

I spat on that word.

Akriti: "Call him psychopath."

She nodded her head silently and together we approached towards the bathroom. There was a small window above my head and the sound was coming from it. We got a chair and I climbed on it, slowly opened the latches and slide the door. It was a proper house and the noise coming from the TV news.

Namrata: "Akriti it is time he will be on his way....come down."

Akriti: "Wait let me see the news."

Namrata: "Come now it is the last hope and I won't let you ruin it."

She was scared and pull me down.

Akriti: "I'm the one who find it you dumb."

I said it in frustration and immediately realized.

Akriti: "Sorry Namrata."

Namrata: "Don't be......"

Namrata: "You are right....you found it. I'm a scary kitten, after all these days if I found this..... It could save me and that girl."

We heard a sound.

Namrata: "He is coming!"

The door was opened and closed with a slam.

Arun: "My....my girls Weldon, you made it a home."

We stand steady and eyes are down. A knife was in my hand and I griped it tight when he walked close to me but truth was I don't have that courage to slit his throat out. The helplessness gave me gilt.

Arun: "Let that knife rest for a while Akriti."

I hold it tightly in fear.

Arun: "I said give it away."

He lunged on me and walloping. Blood smeared from nose, swelling and bruises on face but those nonstop punches and kicks grab more graunch and like a rebellion I hold the knife so tight. A time come he slow down and fall on floor. His face was in front of me. I smiled aggressively, he saw the knife was still in my hand and immediately ran away. Namrata was absolutely dismayed.

Namrata: "What just happened?"

Akriti: "Nothing dear."

Akriti: "I'm too tired and hungry please give me some food."

She tucks me kindly and carefully put me on bed, cleaned the wound and gave me a strong dose of painkiller. Slowly my eyes got down, saw a huge open paddy field. No boundaries, no restrictions, free from plagiarisms. Cows eating fresh grass and following the direction of wind I was running willingly. Golu was holding my hand faithfully and pulling me to the direction of whit beautiful pigeons. Suddenly the sky turned red, paddy field was on fire and Golu changed into Arun.

Akriti: "Golu....."

Namrata: "Are you okay dear?"

Namrata: "Don't worry it's a nightmare."

Juggled a glass of water and about to walk, my left leg gave a killing pain and I set back.

Namrata: "What are you doing Akriti, how could you be so irresponsible!"

She reminds me a bit of my mother.

Namrata: "Is it aching that hard?"

Akriti: "No, manageable."

Namrata: "Why your eyes are sobing?"

Akriti: "You remind me of someone very close to my heart Namrata."

Namrata: "Good for you Akriti."

She was terrible hiding her emotions, tears are running out still got busy in cutting bandages and cleaning my wounds. I can't control it and hugged her tight. After a while she started crying like craving it. I let her hugged until she flushed last ounce of emotion from her heart. Almost a week I was with this unknown girl but it was hard to tell I don't know her. She was telling about her family, chemistry with her little sister. Within every two to three day intervention Arun make us visit but Namrata won't let him touch me. I have seen her got fucked brutally, beaten brutally but at the end a satisfaction on her face that I was unharmed. The guilt swallow me up I'm so helpless protecting my protector but this was the pact she made with me behalf of exchanging friendship. A month went like a blow of wind, police and government still failed to get Arun in custody, crime branch dug into his family history and shockingly Arun was a born criminal. His father was a smuggler, caught by forest rangers a lot of time smuggling elephant teeth, sandal wood, but his good political connection always helped him escape unharmed. He never had ever imagined that he was going to kill by his own son. For more brief information let me take you to the news bulletins. Arun was in his tenth standard, his mother was a simple village woman and like every mother she has dreams to see her son as a successful government officer, and the expectation was righteous. He was a bright student. But Arun have no good relation with his father, they are like Hiranyakashipu and Prahlada. At one angle his father was a crime lord, smuggling, killing, involve in many unsolved rape case and Arun was the good boy of the village. He had a secret crush to Pallavi, his classmate. What he don't know, his father had eye on her from the beginning. One night there was a huge fight between his parents and his mother beaten up to death. Luckily Arun tuck her to hospital and she survived. But tragic lies in the reason. His father tried to convince Pallavi to marry him when she denied he kidnapped her and raped several times, unfortunately he was caught by his wife and before she could stop him he attempted to kill her. The prodigal father broke him inside out. Later his father arrested for his goon activities. Arun waited up to two year for his father. He killed him on the day he got bailed and destroyed the body. Police searched many of his hideouts but failed to get the dead body. They accused Arun but lack of evidence set him free. The villager's were happy finally Hiranyakashipu was dead but what they don't know Prahlada was dead too. Arun become a monster.

Namrata: "And when he offended by you in your school his sleeping beast awaken again."

Akriti: "Correct Namrata."

Akriti: "If I would have the slightest idea whom I'm messing with, Trust me Namrata I never do that."

Namrata: "If we have the power to change the past then I have a lot to change."

Namrata: "You did the right thing, being a teacher is a very noble profession and people like Arun don't deserve to be a teacher."

Akriti: "One second Namrata, he was my teacher but how the acquaintance with you."

Namrata: "He was my tutor and I was under his stewardship."

Akriti: "So did he...."

Namrata: "Yes, Akriti he did."

Namrata: "I was a bright student and his tuition class was famous back then in our town. He was looking innocent and a sober man so father sends me to him without a doubt. For seven months the class went well. Both were focused to purpose. It was after pre-board examination."

Namrata: "He convinced my father for extra classes and a month went well. I was way passionate in my studies, but he was too passionate on my body. At the beginning he touches seductive point but I did ignore him, day by day he was getting more frank and that was unacceptable."

Namrata: "I skipped tuition class and did my studies at home. I was very shameful to discuss it and he tuck the advantage. One day he approached to father and complained about me. I was forced to go back to his classes again. My father doesn't know with whom he was dealing and Arun did play his evil game."

Namrata: "That day he convinced me for extra class, but the part I don't know was he made that arrangement for me only. I was focused on my school homework's, felt someone walking from the behind. The time I wiggled he sprayed chloroform on me and after an hour when I come to conscious I saw, I was on his bed hands and legs are tied and body was naked."

Akriti: "Wait a minute Namrata he raped you when you back to senses."

Namrata: "Yes..."

Akriti: "Fucking prick."

Namrata: "He loved to see people in pain more than sex, it gives him pleasure."

Namrata: "I prayed him....bagged him but his ferocious intentions are not in his control. The story not end that day, he raped me of more two times but when my father come to know about the ideal face of my tutor it was too late. I thought he will understand me give me proper justice but he did exact opposite, collected few of the compromised pictures and other evidences and settled the case."

Akriti: "I know Namrata how it feels when you crocked by your own people."

Namrata: "Why you are asking this Akriti?"

Akriti: "If you want to defeat Arun you should have to know his case study."

Namrata: "And how suppose his past history help us to escape."

Akriti: "Actually it did crime branch went to his village to his mother and...."

Namrata: "And...?"

Akriti: "They got the information of all his hideout."

Namrata: "Are you sure!"

Akriti: "Damn sure darling..... fresh news."

Namrata smiled chirpy.

Namrata: "That's why he stopped visiting us."

Akriti: "Yes Namrata we are the last asset for him."

Akriti: "Government announced shoot on site against him."

Namrata: "That's great Akriti, you just set my mood. Let me prepare a delicious curry for you."

I loved her fanatic smile and addicted with her motherly affection. How God was such cruel for an innocent girl like her. I was thinking of God but devil knocked on the door. Main door latches are opened. We looked each other and involved in household works. Arun entered to the room and found sweet fragrance of the curry. He got alert something is wrong and searched the entire house. Shiv, screwdriver and the weapons he expected are at its place. 'Why girls seemed happy?' Meanwhile Namrata went to him with a glass of water. She smelled something was cooking in his mind and that was not good for us. He tucked the glass and about to drink but suddenly stopped, following a slow sound went to the bathroom and gave a close look to the window above his head. It was slightly opened. I was insanely feared, understood the mistake and prepared to get punished. While he walked to us Namrata stood at front of me but I'm already his target. First he jolted a slap to her, she fell on floor and then he jumped to his prey. He was totally lost control on his mind and walloping me like a maniac. Namrata can't afford to see that and hit his head with crockery. He turned and looked her. She stood still like a brave one. He tucks a knife and about to slit her throat I stabbed his leg with a sharp piece of wood which I did hide for this day. For a moment he stopped like afraid of us. We got confident and attacked his arms. The wooden piece stabbed and jammed in his left arm. He got away to a distance and tuck out a gun from his pocket and pointed to us, a sound of gunfire. We felt someone fall on floor and that was not us. Police had come to rescue us. Before we could judge a bunch of uniformed men entered into the room and make sure he was dead and then covered us in blanket. We interrogated and handover to our family. They are crying hugging us cuddling and kissing us affectionately. We hugged and waved our hands for goodbye. But I never thought it was going to be the last goodbye for Namrata. For next few days I can't say it was great but I can say I was safe in my house, locked away from society and loved by my family. Like the old habit mom came to room with a bottle of coconut oil. I was cherished and like ready for head massage. First few drops of oil she put on my head and involves her magical hands in scratching and rubbing it.

Anita: "Dear I thought totally lost you."

Akriti: "I thought so mom."

Anita: "We never wanted wrong with anyone so why we are the one who always punished by god. First he tucked your dad and now you."

Akriti: "Mom calm down it is nothing to do with God. We did what we can do, but who knows Arun will get bailed and do the conundrum."

Akriti: "Stop talking about it and please it is too tough to forget but I want to cooperate with the flow of time. Please let the topic be silence."

Anita: "I want too dear but not sure the ill minded society will do. They will scratch your wound until it turns into cancer."

Her hands are stopped; I turned and looked to her face. She was dismayed and conjured for an unknown situation.

Akriti: "Why are you crying mom."

Anita: "You know when your father passed away I tuck the decision to do job and that decision laid me a lot of societal trolling and when I got married second time you know very well how our neighbours behaved with us. I don't want that situation for you Akriti, after all you are only seventeen and you survived way lot troubles."

Akriti: "Hey mom, for the name of neighbour what is the update of Ray family, and....."

Anita: "And?"

Anita: "Golu."

A chirpy smile appeared on both of our face.

Anita: "Hmmm.... A few days before they are totally shifted to Mumbay."

Akriti: "Why?"

Anita: "Simple Akriti they want expansion of their business."

Akriti: "Ooooo... and Golu."

Anita: "Yes he called a lot of time and telegrammed few letters but...."

Akriti: "But....what mom?"

Anita: "we didn't answer any of that."

Akriti: "Why?"

Spat on her.

Anita: "Akriti there is no choice we are too busy in our grief."

Anita: "The day I got the news you are alive and unharmed, it was like my sole getting back to the empty husk."

Immediately I hugged her and she tucks me into her arms so tightly. It was warm and very comforting. After the good night head massage I went to the bed and looking out of the window, the moon was looking very beautiful and cold. Slowly eyes are closed. I can feel someone was on the window, straight staring at me like scanning me top to bottom. The door was slowly opened. A shadow stretched towards the bed and elegantly slid into the blanket. I was petrified, helplessly waiting for the catastrophe.

Raman: "Akriti..."

Akriti: "Golu...."

And I woke up.

Everything was as it should be. Solitude and dark. Something felt itchy and I let the light on. There are a few of postcards and letters on the tables, Boston stamps on it. For a moment looked chirpily and tuck all of them to bed and opened it one by one. There are a lot of photographs with every letter he sent to me. I started with the first letter. There was a photograph of a house enveloped with it.

Raman: "Hi love, please don't read my letters in front of your family."

I giggled.

Raman: "If you are reading this then it means I'm safely landed at Boston. I'm sharing the photo of my residency with you. And don't worry about me I'm no loner, there are two musketeers with me. Rani and John. They are taking care of me like a family but still I miss you a lot. I'm sharing with you my telephone number and fax number please call me I'm thrust for your voice."

Immediately unfolded another letter.

Raman: "Hi love, did you miss me? I know you do. I'm writing this because you know very well, I'm terrible keeping secrets and it's urgent because today I caught Rani sneaking upon John. It was difficult for her too but she tucks faith on me and shared her feelings. She has been loved him since the day they mat. And this eejit know nothing about it. It felt me like our story. Last night I was crying pathetic before sleeping. Don't you miss me love."

Two drops of tear fall on the letter and hugged it like feeling his aroma in it. Suddenly looking around the bed and tuck the first letter and searching something carefully.

Akriti: "Got it!"

The phone number sooth me alive and heart beet was pumping so loud in excitement. There are a lot of thoughts drives me creasy. I can feel the adrenalin rush with an unknown but lovely fear. I was about to rotate the dial but stopped. There are a lot of things hacking my mind, 'I will not tell him?' 'No..... I will not.' 'But he deserved to know what I have been through!' 'If he broke up..... then!' 'Let me check what is in his head first?'

Akriti: "Yes.....!"

I was about to dial the number, stopped. This time I herd something from the downstairs. Out of curiosity put the telephone behind and walk in direction of that voice. At the middle of night mom and Kartic uncle was discussing something at kitchen.

Anita: "You can't do this, it is so unwise Kartic."

Kartic: "What is so unwise, we will take care of her expenses."

Anita: "And let her go?"

Kartic: "Yes, Anita."

Anita: "Why Kartic, and where she would go?"

Kartic: "India is a big country."

Answer was too rude for mom and me, tears rolled out but still I like to stay and listen.

Anita: "If our son got in trouble like that what you will do?"

Kartic: "He will not I make sure Akriti will stay away from him."

Anita: "Ooooo....... this is the reason, you want him out of her shadow."

Anita: "Tell me Kartic is it her fault that some freak fucking libido kidnapped her for his self amusement?"

Kartic: "I don't know Anita, what I know is my son need a better life. With her this is impossible."

It was just the beginning, quarrelling, fighting, beating are become the alternative communication between mom and Kartic uncle. Concurrently there were a lot of rumours troubled me to get a good character certificate, apparently getting an admission in a college was way difficult for me. Wherever I do go people ogling me like I was a characterless prostitute. These cunt approaches, saes conversations kept mom pushing to ill health and depression. Day by day my life went more difficult but hope is the remedy to every illness. The thought went wrong when one morning I found a letter, it was from Namrata. I rip the envelope in excitement and went to room. Firstly I let my anxiety calm and opened the envelope.

Namrata: "Dear Akriti I hope you are doing well, Still remember the first-time I saw you in the cage of that ogre. A true combination of beauty and simplicity. The confusion and fear on your face always force me to take care of you and your irresistible affection..... I tried tough but can't escape it. Nonetheless lovely smile on your face..... always a priceless gift for me. In that few moments

I spend with you..... you let me become your mother, sister and a dear friend. Thank you for giving me that honour."

I smiled affirmative and focused on next paragraph.

Namrata: "Now come to the point, You realized already the trouble society giving to us even after knowing that we are the victim. Like you I did try my best to get a character certificate, knocked door of plenty of high profile people. Thought that time to forget the past and walk to a new life full of education and wisdom but who ever I did approach for the help they only seek me in their bed. Everyday I saw my father coming back to home dwindled, hopeless and shameful; I can't let my bad reputation consume my family. I can't let my sisters life spoiled beneath my bad reputation."

My eyes stunned on the letter like going to read something worst, scared.

Namrata: "If you are reading this then it is conformed I'm resting in peace. See you in afterlife love, stay strong and be brave."

The letter flipped from my hand and bumped on the floor. Before tears can satisfy my emotion I heard a painful crying from the downstairs. A thought of menacing push me to go. The baby was in one hand and other hand was piled with luggage. Mom was standing in front of him, bagging, crying, quarrelling but he had no reason to see her at least once. Like a stubborn Kartic uncle walked into the taxi. Before the madding grows to more frown I kept hugged mom until the car all off from my site. After an hour of crying mom got fainted. I was scared 'do I have to take care of mom or do grief on the situation I did obtain.' I play guile and telephoned the doctor. After a thorough check-up it was conformed she was suffered a heavy mental stress

and I was the only responsible for her misery. The doctor had guided me the medicines and worn me not to disturb her or not speak something which trigger her stress again.

Doctor: "Dear I'm telling this to you not as a doctor, I'm her friend and I can't see your mother like this."

I had nothing more than a faint smile to pay her. She waved her hand on my head like a blessing and kissed forehead. The only word repeatedly hammering my mind was 'friend' and last words of Namrata was whispering in my ears. Finally the doctor had gone and I found a golden opportunity to end my life, but instantly all my ill thoughts were vanished when I saw sleeping innocent face of mom.

Akriti: "Mom had fighting all alone for me, lose love of her life and her son. What she will do when I die."

That thought only bring tears in my eyes, it was cruelly selfish to end my misery at once. All the daylong didn't moved from her site, a girl who was symbol of nonsense now cooking and take care for the house and her mother. It's a week now reluctantly I was visiting colleges for an admission but failure was in my faith. The only good news I have was mom recovering faster. I got my strength back. It was one evening after waiting all day long in the local MLA office I had back to home. A smooth fragrance of food all around the house. The messy kitchen was arranged properly, cushions are at their place. It gave me a feeling of my school days. Following the aroma I walked to the dining table, like the old days food was served on the table.

I grinned;

Akriti: "Mom...mom...mo..."

Akriti: "Let me yum, I'm so starving."

It tucks me only fifteen minutes to wipe up the plate. Few rice grains are on my lips showing respect for her effort in cooking and a smile which I forgot a long time ago.

Akriti: "Mom where are you?"

Akriti: "Mom...."

That was the last time I called her name desperately. The situation was too upsetting when I saw her lifeless body hanging and swinging below the roof in her room. The confidence and a glimpse of self-respect all gone, within an hour a pile of gathering including police coming in and out. People are looking at my misery like a live telecast. I was still dismayed, disappointed and dwindled in between reality and my thoughts. Her body was taken into the ambulance. Suddenly a pain induced in my heart and I cried hollered, run after her like a lunatic.

Akriti: "She is mine....she is mine."

Akriti: "Take off your filthy hands fucking pricks."

Akriti: "She wanted to stay with me."

Akriti: "Mom why can't you tell them how much you love me...."

Two police constable tuck off my hands forcefully over her body and hold me until the ambulance disappear. A day after that the post-mortem report and the dead body was handover to me. According to the report mom died because of choking of the wind pipe but the struggle which put her into this cowardly action, there is no explanation of it. No one, even Kartic uncle avoid attending the funeral. Few days went in grief and sorrow put me in a position of gravely depression. Several time suicidal thoughts were hung up on my mind, finally one day at noon a white Ambassador car was stopped near my house. It stayed up to five hours and that five hour changed my life totally. It was the local MLA came to give me a helping hand on behalf of a barter to satisfy him on bed. After that night my whole life was changed. I got a new name 'Rose Madam', became a high profile prostitute and an ambition of a lot of high-profile men. Get the character certificate and admission in one of the finest college, Revensa. It was the biggest lesson in my life 'if you want a character certificate from society! First you have to become characterless.' The days went by, I abdicated way much wealth and seas enough power to call myself powerful. No more pity, no more bagging. Always an expression of cunning smile on my face. Being in limelight was a habit of my daily routine and swindling hearts of rich men was the job. A lot of innocent families were destroyed because of my honey trap but who cares I have my own luxury car to attend college which was even dream for a rich kid, the part I underestimated 'every story has its end and mine was necessary to end.' One day afternoon I drive back from college to the home a sudden dizziness appeared before the eyes and after a short amnesia everything gone dark.

Nurse: "Ma'am.....ma'am. Akriti ma'am."

A slow and sweet voice bring me back to the mortal world. Few hospital staff was surrounding me. It tucks me a while to understand my exact location. Plenty of machines were attached to me and people around my bed looking at me like I was an animal from zoo. Again a headache and feeling of Amnesia.

Akriti: "Where am I?"

Doctor: "Don't worry dear you are in safe hands."

The doctor said sweetly.

Doctor: "It has been a month you were in coma. We found you from a car crash. Luckily your car has good safety features and unluckily your expensive car is crippled..... Akriti."

The doctor looked happy seeing me alive like I'm dearer to him. Putting an ailing smile on face I looked down, left leg was broken, few fingers of my hands broken too. Cuts and bruises were all around the body.

Akriti: "Water..."

Doctor: "Oooo....yes Akriti I will make that arrangement for you."

Saying that doctor has followed way out.

***

DOP switched and the stage gone brighter. Audience was looking to us like there is more to speak, I thought that too. But Kathrin was not. Tears are rolling down; eyes are full of gilt and sorrow. She won't make it anymore and walked to the backstage.

Raman: "Sorry for the inconvenience, we will meet tomorrow same time with your dear storyteller Raman Ray. Thank you."

With a jittery smile on my face I tried my best to restore the interest but audience already lacked their attention and escaped from the gallery one by one. I managed the goodbye speech and immediately walked to the backstage. Kathrin was seating in dressing room and looking to the mirror like pity on her.

Raman: "What is it Kathrin, how you can be so unprofessional, you know how difficult it is to cover up a conundrum on stage. I saw them dissatisfied and inconvenient."

She looked to my lips until they stop moving and kissed. I can't stop my intentions too and snagged her like waiting for it. That night the wheel of time revert again, rain was out bursting and inside the bedroom we hop on each other like a wild animal, loving irresistibly. Sometimes she clings on and some time I do. Clothes were all over the floor, finally we immersed in one another's arm. The night was still young and rain drops make it wet. I was moving my hands softly around her neck and she was looking me like I was her precious jewel.

Raman: "That dress!"

Kathrin: "Yes?"

Raman: "I gave you on our first date."

Kathrin: "yes Raman.....you noticed?"

She seems delighted and kissed like owned me. That taste of her lips tuck me back to the Boston school of law. I was seating near the lawn and holding an ice bag on my swelling face.

John: "Wooo.... your brother-in-law is so nasty."

Raman: "Drop it John. I'm not in the mood."

Rani: "you two again."

Entered at the moment.

Raman: "He started."

John: "I didn't Rani, only worried about him."

Rani: "John stop that puppy face I'm not your mom. And you owe an apology to him. Say it like a good boy."

John: "I'm sorry Raman."

Raman: "Its okay."

We smiled funnily and hugged. A beautiful black Mercedes stopped and Kathrin alighted. Seeing us she headed to the lawn.

Kathrin: "Aren't you guys having classes to attend."

John: "Not really!"

He said with an obligation. Kathrin looked to him fishy.

John: "Can you explain the damage done to my dearest friends face."

I saw him in anger.

Kathrin: "Yes it is... I'm sorry to take you to my favourite spot. I should be more precautious."

Raman: "There is no need of it Kathrin, now to the point we need to do something about it."

Rani: "He is correct Kathrin!"

Kathryn: "You don't have to worry about it, aunt Lee already tuck care of it."

Raman: "How?"

I was worried.

Kathryn: "I knew Tom will take this matter to him."

Raman: "Your papa Mr.Norman knew all this."

Kathryn: "Yes...."

Raman: "God help me!"

Raman: "What I suppose to do now?"

Kathryn: "Nothing you have to come."

Raman: "For what?"

Kathryn: "Dinner."

She said it so cutely.

Raman: "With your father?"

Kathryn: "Of course it is."

John: "Dear Kathrin what have you done?"

He got tension.

John: "It's time to all off Raman."

Kathryn: "I think you guys taking it too much, papa know you as my good friend. I told you Aunt Lee already had it under her control."

Raman: "Never mind I need some air."

And next moment I was standing in front of Mr.Norman. I was invited for the dinner. After college Kathrin tuck me with her to home. 'Home is actually not suitable, a palace is more preferable.' For a second I got intimated looking into the foods on dining table.

Mr.Norman: "Son!"

Raman: "Sir!"

Mr.Norman: "Please have a seat, I prefer uncle then sir."

Raman: "Of cores sir.....sorry....uncle."

Kathrin tucks the next seat behind me which was quit backstabbing for Tom. I can realize looking into his grumpy face. The feast has begun.

Mr.Norman: "I herd that you are a good story teller?"

Raman: "Not really uncle."

Mr.Norman: "Don't be shy son, I always appreciate talent but with one condition and that is you should know how to make profit out of it."

Kathrin: "Papa...."

Kathrin said it with an embarrassment.

Mr.Norman: "What is your future plan son, how you plan to get bread and butter?"

The conversation went little deep which was a moment of enjoyment for Tom. I looked into silent white face of Mr.Norman.

Raman: "Uncle....after the LAW."

Mr.Norman: "LAW?"

Raman: "Yes!"

Mr.Norman: "Tom.... when you're going to tell me he is a law student."

Mr.Norman: "I'm sorry son, apology. I thought you are a literature and arts student."

Kathrin: "He is among the top 10 papa."

Said it proudly.

Mr.Norman: "Delighted."

Mr.Norman: "Truly son. You are interesting, so how you two get acquainted."

Kathrin, Raman: "In college campus."

We said it at once. Mr. Norman saw us ambitiously. I understood my first impression put that charm on his face but Kathrin looked worried. She learned her father better than me. One side daughter and another side was father and at the middle me a conflict. I choose a better option the plate full of butter chicken and the vintage wine.

Kathrin: "Check your phone."

Raman: "Okay?"

Kathrin: "After meal papa will invite you to his private tavern. He will start with the sweet interrogation and continue the conversation until he let your true self out. Be aware of the conundrum. Do not let him into your head."

Mr.Norman: "Son!"

Raman: "Sir?"

Mr.Norman: "No...sir."

Raman: "Sorry, uncle."

Mr.Norman: "I hope you enjoyed the meal."

Raman: "Truly....fantastic."

Mr.Norman: "Don't spoil that word. If you really see something fantastic come with me I have a private bar and a sacred place where man can talk to a man."

I looked behind. Kathrin was waving her head in worry like she wanted to say 'just say no.'

Mr.Norman: "Why not it is my privilege to talk with you in person."

Tom was smiling seeing all this drama like he knew what his father going to do with me and waved his hand like saying goodbye to me until the door has closed.

Now I was own my own. I looked around, the place was magnificent.

Mr.Norman: "Magnificent isn't it. Come son, grab a seat."

He can read the nervousness in my eyes, and I can see a demonic smile on his face. A bartender walked to us, He looked smart, probably more than me and his eyes are looking only me like I was there for a sacrifice.

Mr.Norman: "What you like to order son."

Raman: "Apple juice....probably!"

Voice was jittery.

Mr.Norman: "Nice joke....ha..ha..ha....nice one, Hit the stage hard."

The bartender understood and prepared two drinks for us.

Mr.Norman: "Let me tell you the rules, you have to bottom up the drink at once."

Raman: "Okay!"

Mr.Norman: "Whom you're waiting for, cheers."

It was all normal at the beginning, but slowly eyes got numb, everything including Mr.Norman was floating around me. In short a godly feeling possessed my mind.

Mr.Norman: "Tell me son where are you from?"

Raman: "India."

Mr.Norman: "Native?"

Raman: "Odisha."

Mr.Norman: "Good....how many people are in your family?"

Raman: "Including me my mom and dad."

Mr.Norman: "Have you ever been in any relationship?"

Raman: "Yes."

Mr.Norman: "When?"

Raman: "At school."

Mr.Norman: "Odisha!"

Raman: "Yes."

Mr.Norman: "What is her name?"

Raman: "Akriti."

Mr.Norman: "I see......is she better than my daughter?"

Raman: "Yes!"

Mr.Norman: "Are you sure?"

Raman: "I don't know."

Mr.Norman: "Good."

Mr.Norman: "So you guys are still in touch...right!"

Raman: "No....not anymore."

Mr.Norman: "Okay, tell me about your father?"

Raman: "He is a good man, love me a lot....do call me twice a day and always appreciate my efforts."

Mr.Norman: "What is he doing for living?"

Raman: "Hmmm......"

My eyes gone blurred and I can't see his face anymore. Only a blind voice kept me go on.

Mr.Norman: "Son....son are you listening?"

Raman: "Ha..ha....yes I'm."

Mr.Norman: "I repeat....what does your father do?"

Raman: "He....is a lawyer."

Mr.Norman: "Tell me more."

Raman: "He owned an ancestral law firm... 'The Ray Law Firm.' One of the finest and oldest company which solved a pile of high profile cases in India."

Mr.Norman: "You are son of Raghab and Smita Ray?"

He got mesmerized.

Raman: "Yes sir."

Saying that I did vomit all on the face of Mr.Norman and after a short cloudy vision everything was dark. The morning was very much hectic, the pain was too much in my head like someone hammering my mind and hangover gave a different type of pain to my body. In middle of that phone was ringing. It was papa.

Raghab: "How you doing son?"

Raman: "Good morning papa."

I said it awfully.

Raghab: "Still that hangover headache is in you?"

Raman: "Yes! How you know that?"

Raghab: "That drink is way tough."

Raman: "How?"

Saying that the last vision came to my mind, the way I did vomit on Mr.Norman, it was totally irresistible.

Raman: "Leave it, I have a pile of questions for you papa."

Raghab: "Yes, I know. I helped Mr.Norman to settle his business in India. By that time I worked for another law firm and he was the client. He found spark in me and many times he tried to convince me to work with him but when I tuck the responsibility of our ancestral law business we became a forever friend and a loyal partner to each other."

Raman: "That's sweet of you papa."

Raghab: "That was the only reason I put you in Boston. When time come I myself going to introduce you to him but I think it is too early."

Someone came into room Un-invited and snatched the phone, very unfriendly.

Mr.Norman: "Nothing is ever too soon Ray you fucking basted."

Raghab: "Norman my friend....please control your emotions, my son is still there."

Mr.Norman: "Its fine, he is young enough to listen these words."

Raghab: "Ha..ha..ha. You're never going to change frivolous freak."

Mr.Norman: "Some people remain classy you know. Okay I talked too much."

Saying that he gave the phone to me.

Raman: "Bye....papa."

I put the phone on table and looking to his eyes unconvincingly. Mr.Norman was smiling exact like the last night. It put me into a slight tension 'what is cooking in his mind now.'

Mr.Norman: "Nothing is cooking in my mind son, I'm only curious seeing a Ray in my house and I know nothing about it."

He said like reading my mind.

Mr.Norman: "Son I need to apologize. The behaviour truly immature but love for my daughter is true. I know she is a smart girl but I can't control my father instinct. I think you understand!"

Raman: "Yes, uncle now I totally understand."

We both laughed at once and the door was opened. Kathrin walked in worried. She doesn't want her father to conduct another stupid experiment on me. So do I. After a glass of lemon juice I feel better and together we went to the college. Tom was not a thon for us anymore and our love express put the throttle at its optimum speed 'condition applied, this train has no stoppage or any full-stop.' With a blink of eye years blown away and Rani, John, Kathrin and I became a cult. The togetherness kept our bond strong and forever. The only trouble I had was how I can compile my creative self and professional self, but my girlfriend has an idea regarding that. 'Our parents only need good grades from our academic carrier and I'm already good at it. I only have to find a good part-time creative job.' So did I. After a long time I got a fulfilment in my life. Perfect friends, perfect girlfriend who stands with me in my up and downs, a desired part-time radio jockey job help me in touch with my passion of story telling and with bonus point I learned story writing too. The best part my parents are happy for my academic carrier in Boston Law School. Sounds like a happy ending.

＊＊＊

I woke up with a stress phone call from the hospital, Kathrin was worried more than me. When we arrived Ronith was waiting at outdoor.

Ronith: "Raman...."

Raman: "Ronith...."

His worried face tucks me to the day I met him in Boston. It was a usual Saturday for me and as per schedule all four of us were gathered near Starbucks after college, doing the friendly nonsense and drinking the coffee. Suddenly I felt someone was staring at me and I looked to that direction. A man was seating alone wearing a black cap and drinking coffee. The body language reminds me of someone and suspicious too. When he saw I was marching forward to him, he got aware and rapidly collected his gears from table, but it was too late for him.

Raman: "Ronith....."

I said out of anxiousness.

Ronith: "Yes I'm and I know you very well too, Raman Ray."

He said it so cold, not in a mood to meet me.

Raman: "How are you?....what are you doing here?..... what you do for living? Don't you feel ask questions like this."

Ronith: "Not really Raman."

Again a cold expression in his eyes.

Raman: "Okay then let me start with these questions."

Ronith: "Studying MBBS, and I'm here because of an internship and Raman if you want to know more follow me to my apartment."

There was a pain in his voice pushed me to follow him. All this happens to me like a fiction novel. Finding a school rival all of a sudden and he was lurking at you all the time quit interesting.

Ronith: "After you Raman."

The apartment was well arranged and a fragrance which was very close to my heart. Everything felt sacred. My phone was banging continuously.

Ronith: "Take that call Raman, Kathrin must be worried."

Raman: "How do you know about her? Are you spying on me? Look what we were at school that was childish, I have nothing to do with you now."

He was listening till I shut my mouth and then pushed a bear bottle.

Ronith: "You need this; whatever I'm going to tell you it needs to focus and patience. So please seat down."

He told me everything from the day I left Odisha till he ended up with Akriti at hospital when she was severely injured in a car crash. The bear bottle was still on table straight in front of my eyes. I looked to it for a second and bottom up at once.

Raman: "I need another one."

Said it grumpily

Ronith: "Yes Raman."

Ronith: "She was here, staying with me."

Raman: "So you both are in relationship?"

Ronith: "No Raman I'm her doctor."

I looked him in a questionable expression.

Ronith: "She is suffering from leukaemia stage three."

The bear bottle fall from my hand.

Raman: "So then she was here for the treatment."

Ronith: "No she wishes to die from the beginning but she wanted you to be dead before hers."

Raman: "What?"

Ronith: "Yes dear friend she was here to put a bullet in your head."

Ronith: "Did you ever felt intrusions like you saw her!"

Raman: "Yes I tried to follow her but didn't."

Ronith: "She was there......to kill you, I was there too."

Raman: "what then?"

Ronith: "She can't make it."

Raman: "Why? And why she wanted me dead at first place?"

Ronith: "Akriti can't kill you because she saw love and pain in your eyes that day and why she wanted you dead? You should need to ask that to your mother."

Raman: "Ronith you are making it complicated."

Ronith: "Isn't it fishy your parents moved to Mumbai when Akriti was kidnapped. Okay if this evidence is not good enough then tell me did you ever try to know about Akriti and your parents avoided it!"

Raman: "Yes a lot of time. Can you speak freely Ronith?"

Spat on him.

Ronith: "Okay, then listen. Your mother was solely responsible for disrupting her life."

Raman: "Take that back Ronith. You don't know what you are talking."

Ronith: "I'm actually. You and Akriti both put all your effort to see Arun behind the bar but did you ever realize how he got bailed so easily, his family have no capacity to get him out, so who did it?"

I was silently waiting for his conclusion.

Ronith: "Your mother did it."

Raman: "How could you be so sure?"

Ronith: "I'm not dear friend, Akriti has the photo copy of the bail papers and your mother's signature on it."

A sound of door opened and I woke up from my daydream. The doctor has arrived and called me to meet him in his office. It was already night fall and hospital was looking like a ghost house. Strange noises were breaking through the silence corridor. Ronith and Kathrin both were sleeping on the couch. I did follow the doctor to his office. I was too much nervous.

Doctor: "Raman please take the seat."

Raman: "Thanks doctor."

Doctor: "Now what I'm going to tell you......please listen to me carefully."

Raman: "You are looking nervous doctor....what happened?"

Doctor: "What I'm going to tell you, please don't take me wrong."

Raman: "Yes.....okay."

Doctor: "Akriti has been doing this since your book has published."

Raman: "She has been doing what?"

I was little drifted.

Doctor: "Aaaa....look I tried to stop her a lot of time."

Raman: "Doctor please start from the beginning, so I can relate."

Doctor: "Raman tell me did she pushed you to start over a fresh life or involve in a relationship."

Raman: "Yes she is, A lot of time I had disagreed on this topic. Why are you asking?"

Doctor: "Akriti has done call upon her health intentionally."

Raman: "What that suppose to mean?"

Doctor: "Please check your phone Raman You will get all answer." Saying that the doctor has left the room. After a short silence unlocked the phone. There was a fresh email revealing on the dashboard. It was a series of videos and I waited until it downloaded. Hesitation clearly reflected in my eyes.

Akriti: "Hi Golu, Akriti here. You are thinking why this video. Because I'm going to tell you something which I can't speak in person. Strange right."

Clicked another video.

Akriti: "If you are seeing this I probably dead. Please don't do any nonsense until I end talking, it is my last request. I know the exact situation you are in, eyes were bursting out of tears, hands are shaking, running nose. Hey one thing is missing, did someone tell you that your nose got red when you are crying. My pore cry baby ha... ha...ha."

I can't bare the pain of my heart, it was pinching so hard and I went to the next video.

Akriti: "Hoooo..... enough hooey talks, time to be serious. A while ago one of my dear friend send me a suicide letter and told me to not give up, bounce back, fight back or what ever. But I didn't......I didn't keep my promise. I galloped in a wrong way for seeking my revenge from society. The part I forgot was 'when you through a rock to a mud, few splashes of dirt will bounce back and make your dress muddy too.' Destroyed a lot of life's, houses and a plenty of lovers were severed because of me."

Akriti: "I understand that when I end up in a car crash. There I learned I was suffering from leukaemia. A huge melancholy laughter on my face. Thank God I found Ronith out there. Soon he learned my situations.....I thought now to move on but I was wrong. Despite all odds he stood for me, and helped me to get out of my past. But past have scars remain on our body. One of my associate one day gave me an envelope. It was a photocopy of a bail paper Signed by your mother for Arun sir. The aftermath was revealed and revenge blinded me again. I landed at Boston to kill you."

Akriti: "But God have his own way to play with us. I can still see that day, You were in front of window looking out somewhere. I have a pistol in my pocket and you were an easy target at that moment, but I hesitated when our eyes mate. I saw who you are to me. All those grouches were vanished, the remain was pure love for you."

Akriti: "I spend a couple of time around you like your shadow and saw how Kathrin turned your upset life into heavenly happiness, you are fulfilled with everything. Finally I realized time to go and choose Mumbai for my remaining days of life but who wandered one day you will come to me and knock on the door like an angel. I have no words seeing you next to me like my wishes were finally blessed but when I realized you left everything for me, shocked. What have you done? You put your innocent life into an endless misery."

Akriti: "I had to make a decision quickly and it was clear I'm not the one who takes your house down. Back then Kathrin was way deep in trouble. Out of the line, disappointed, depressed and already in a row to carve her name in suicide list. She is really passionate for you Raman."

I tuck a pose, wipe the tears and then played the video.

Akriti: "'If you can't find your love the way you wanted then a time will come your love will find you in another way'. She loves you the way I loved you. The evidence was way enough for me. Finally found a wooden raft in the middle of a deadly ocean. I told her everything and wanted an immediate action but she is the one who want to see you as a successful author."

At the middle of video I herd someone was crying helplessly. It was too late when I arrived, Ronith was seating behind the bed speech less, Kathrin was crying holding her hand and Akriti was sleeping lifeless on the bed, a satisfactory smile on her face 'finally death wish of a bad girl has accomplished.'